C000145557

FATED FOR THE BEAR

BANFORD & BEAUTY BEARS

MINA CARTER

NEW YORK TIMES & USA TODAY BESTSELLING AUTHOR

Copyright © 2018 by Mina Carter

All rights reserved.

No part of this book may be reproduced in any form or by any electronic or mechanical means, including information storage and retrieval systems, without written permission from the author, except for the use of brief quotations in a book review.

CONTENTS

CHAPTER 1

*H*is life sucked, and not in a good way.

At the high-pitched feminine giggles coming from the other side of the bar, Dean Sterling resolutely kept his attention on the beer in his hand. Thirteen of its buddies lined the bar in front of him, but he was no closer to smashed out of his face drunk than when he'd started a couple of hours ago. Pity. He sighed. It would take more than fourteen bottles of weak-assed crap like this to render a *werebear* even mildly tipsy... like maybe a tanker or three.

Werebears, especially alphas like Dean, didn't get drunk easily. Like most shifters, their metabolisms ran too fast for alcohol to have much effect, which was a good thing since bears often made really bad drunks. Pissy was not the word. And Dean wasn't *just* an alpha, he was an alpha among alphas... a Prime, leader of his clan.

Yet here he was in a grubby little backwater bar trying, and failing, to get smashed out of his face. Over a woman, of all things. But then, when was it ever anything different? Women and taxes, the two great banes of any man's life.

He tipped his head back, poured what was left in the bottle down his throat then set the empty down next to its fellows. Without a word, Ash, owner and head barman of the Beast Bar, slid another across the bar.

Most customers, even bears from the local clan, Dean's clan, he would have asked if they'd had enough... but he'd seen the look on Dean's face often enough to know two things—to not ask questions and to keep the alcohol flowing. Preferably until Dean face-planted through alcohol and sheer exhaustion... which was the only way he got any sleep when this mood was upon him.

Despite all the other noises in the bar, the sound of female giggles and the click of pool balls were all he could hear. Every ounce of his attention was focused on the two women on the other side of the bar.

Correction, *one* of the two women on the other side of the bar. As an alpha, Dean was as highly sexed as the rest of them, but even he didn't do multiples, especially when one of the women in question was a mean-assed she-bear. Lilly Braun was an enforcer with the Beauty Clan... Dean's head enforcer. She made sure everyone toed the line and obeyed the rules.

Even he wouldn't cross her, especially if she was in a bad mood. Those days he tended to step lightly and find some clan work right the other side of the territory, that or send her out on patrol. She'd like nothing better than to tear him a new one, even if he was Prime. Sometimes he thought, *especially* because he was Prime. No one was above the law. Not even him. Another sigh hit him and he downed half the new beer in one long swallow.

No, all his attention was on the little human female with Lilly. Kacie Leroy—a pint-sized firecracker of a beauty who had haunted his dreams day and night since he'd figured out the difference between little boys and little girls. Unfortunately, his father, the previous Prime, had chosen that same time to point out the differences between little boy bears and little human girls... And the law said any human that found out about them had to die.

Therein lay the problem. Kacie was human. He was a bear. If he told her what he was, he had to mate her or she had to die. And if he revealed himself as the proverbial monster from legend, he wasn't sure she'd want anything to do with him.

Catch-fucking-twenty-two.

"You know," Ash's voice broke through his musings. "You could just haul her out into the woods, get furry and then get your freak on."

Dean snorted, almost spraying beer through his nose to cover the bar. "Yeah, right! You've met Lilly? If I even *try* that, she'll tear me a fucking new one. Several in fact. She wants me to *talk* to her."

"Hmmm." Ash wrinkled his nose, looking over the bar toward the two women in question. Dean's gaze followed, and for a second he allowed himself the luxury of admiring Kacie's curvy ass as she bent over to take a shot. Her dark hair was upswept, revealing the sensuous curve of her neck and shoulders as her arm came back. A sharp movement later there was the distinctive click of balls colliding and she caroled in triumph, obviously having gotten one up on her opponent.

Dean shivered as she moved, the little head south of his belt taking them on a fantasy joyride of other ways he'd enjoy that view.

Which was right about the point the two men became aware of Lilly watching them. Her eyes dark with her bear, her expression brooked no argument, stating plainly that both had better find something more interesting to look at if they knew what was good for them... Like the ceiling, or maybe the floor.

"Yeah... See what you mean, Capt'n," Ash muttered with a shudder. He wasn't a bear, but a werepanther, and a veteran at that, so he was no slouch. "Wouldn't like to tangle with that one in a hurry."

"Nope. Believe me, you wouldn't." Dean polished off his beer and put it on the bar as the girls finished their game. Seeing Kacie rack her cue and walk toward the ladies' room, Dean took his chance.

Sliding off the bar stool, he sauntered across the bar. The she-bear watched him every step of the way, her expression unreadable. Even though she was one of his kind, one of his clan, and as a bear owed allegiance to him, Kacie was her friend. More than that, they were *best friends* and, in some ways, that trumped his claim.

Especially in this.

"You ready to bear up and tell her?" she growled in demand, not bothering to make sure her voice was entirely human now that the only human in the bar was out of the room.

He winced at her comment. He knew what she meant, and she knew he knew what she meant.

Kacie was his fated mate. The one woman in the world meant for him... and she was human. The fates either had a weird ass sense of humor or they were just fucking bitches. Since he and Kacie lived in the same town, and he'd had to watch her growing up... watch her blossom into a beautiful young woman right under his nose, flirt with all the local boys and he couldn't do a thing about it, he was going with the second option.

Lilly though, didn't see the problem. All he had to do was bring Kacie in, tell her about weres and the bear clan in town, and convince her she was his soul mate. Simple.

Yeah...right.

Kacie was the most grounded person he knew, one who had no tolerance for "fairy stories" as she called them. She'd rip him a new one and then tell him to fuck off and grow up. If he changed in front of her, the scales would be ripped from her eyes and not in a good way. She was strong... but he'd seen hardened combat veterans lose it when faced with the truth. He didn't want that for Kacie.

"We've been through this. Not happening." He didn't stop his bear deepening his voice, a subtle reminder that while they might have been in the middle of a human town, she was still one of his bears. "You two going out tonight?"

She nodded, not bothering to argue. There was no point. Everyone in town knew that the two girls went dancing at the nightclub just out of town on a Friday night. The last Friday of the month, the place would be packed, everyone pouring in from all the towns in the area. Packed with men... human men... men that Kacie might find attractive. And he wanted that, he really did. Or so he told himself. He *should* want that. Should want her to find a nice *safe* human man to settle down with.

But fuck that... the growl rose from the pit of his soul, man and bear in perfect agreement.

"Look after her," he ordered. "Or I'll have your hide for the lodge wall."

Two weeks later...

"Seriously? You told Cast-iron Balls Braun you'd have her hide for the wall?" Morgan Jones, master warlock, combat veteran and all round badass, managed to keep a straight face for all of two point four seconds. Then he burst into laughter, tears streaming down his face. "I always said you were fucking suicidal. Or was that just stupid?"

"Screw you, asshole." Dean chuckled, leaning back in his chair to rub a hand over his short-cropped hair. He and Morgan went way back to their first days in basic, and sometimes he needed the leveler the guy produced on a regular basis.

The two sat in lounge chairs either side of the large fireplace in the Prime's private quarters. Despite the warmth of the season, a small fire crackled merrily in the grate.

"Love you too."

Morgan lounged back and took a sip from the heavy tumbler in his hand. Whiskey, neat. It could be cheap-ass shit or the finest vintage. The warlock didn't care. All went down the same way. Despite the large amount of alcohol the pair had consumed though, his gaze was sharp and perceptive.

"So... when are you going to admit you're fucked six ways to Sunday?"

Dean stared right back. "No clue what you mean."

The warlock rolled his eyes. "Really? You're going with denial? You do know that's only a..."

"...river in Egypt." Dean chuckled. "Yeah, I know."

He leaned his head back and closed his eyes. He had to talk to someone not a bear and not human, and since Morgan was neither, he was it. "And, yes, I know I'm fucked. Totally. My fated mate is a human and half my clan are freaking elitist who believe we should take over the town and make all humans our slaves. Because shit like that's *really* gonna fly in the twenty-first century."

Morgan emptied his glass. "Always did say you bears were a bit slow on the uptake. Apart from Braun... that girl's fine as hell."

Dean's grin was sly. "I'll tell her you said that. She's always had a thing for non-bear paras."

Morgan's expression froze, the look in his eyes somewhere between '*oh hell no*' and '*holy crap.*' "Don't you freaking dare, Sterling, or forget being a bear, I'll turn you into a frog for a month."

Dean just gave a little beckoning motion with his fingers. He'd been turned into worse before. Like that time in the ass end of beyond when Morgan had turned the whole section into weasels so they could get behind enemy lines. He hadn't stopped itching for fucking weeks. Turned out he was allergic to weasel fur.

"And that is my cue to make like a tree and leave."

Morgan heaved himself out of the comfortable chair with a sigh and placed his empty glass on the coffee table. "Don't worry. I can see myself out."

"Don't let the door burn you in the ass on the way out." Dean waved in the direction of the fire.

Morgan's answer was to give him a one-fingered salute as he started to chant, drawing magical sigils in the air over the flames.

They both started a little when the shrill ring of a cell phone split the air. Dean frowned and patted his pockets until he located the thing. The number on the screen made him frown. He punched the answer button and lifted it to his ear.

"What the hell, Braun? I told you guys I was busy tonight."

Even as he spoke, he motioned to Morgan to hold fire. Instantly, the warlock dismissed the transportation spell and waited, gaze and posture ones of alertness.

"Uhm, I'm sorry. Lilly told me to call...that you could help." The voice on the other end of the line was not the one Dean expected. It was soft and breathy. And human.

Icy tendrils of unease wrapped around his spine. Shit, this was not good. He frowned, trying to work out what was going on from the muffled background noises.

"What happened?"

"...Jumped. Secure... alley... get a truck... going to need to move her..."

Dean's heart almost stopped. That was Braun's voice. Who were they moving?

"Hello? Hello? Are you still there?"

"Yeah, I'm here."

The woman came back, but he could hear the fear in her voice.

He dropped his voice to a soothing tone. "Good. Who is this..." The penny dropped. The caller wasn't Braun, or Kacie, and female. Which only left... "Kait, is that you? Kait Turner?"

"Yeah, it is."

"Kaitlyn. I need you to tell me what happened."

It took all his control for Dean to remain calm and not bark orders down the phone. Kait wasn't one of his bears, so he couldn't. Besides, she sounded on the edge of hysteria and, in his experience, pushing would just make her shut down. He'd get no useful information out of her. Like what the hell had happened.

Morgan hovered, his expression intent as he

waited for information. There were no questions, not yet, they'd worked together too often for that.

"There were men." She paused and he heard a hint of movement around her. Heavy footsteps. Not female ones, unless they wore hobnail boots. Within a second or so, Kait spoke again. "Men in the alley, waiting for us. They had...they had claws."

Dean's heart almost stopped. The three girls—Lilly, Kacie and Kait—had always gone out dancing of a weekend when they were younger. Kait had been away for a few years in the city but the other two had continued the tradition. Now Kait was back, and it appeared she'd slipped right back into the routine.

Which also meant he had a good idea where they were. There was only one place on their route they could have been jumped. By men with claws. His blood grew cold, his bear roaring for release.

Bears. They'd been attacked by bears.

"Oh god, there's so much blood."

Before he could ask anything else, there was the sound of movement from the other end of the line and a new voice spoke. Deep with bear tones and male, it was instantly familiar.

"Prime? It's Bennett. We got a couple of intruders. Five by the smell of it. They caught Braun and her friends in the alley by the library. One got tagged and it's bad."

Fear struck his heart like a lance. He'd heard the phrase used before and always scoffed at it for being too fanciful and flowery. But as he sagged forward, his arms numb with the pain, he realized it absolutely felt like someone had jammed a six-foot spike of metal right through his body. So much so, he actually had to flick a glance over his shoulder to ensure no one had snuck into the room behind him and attacked. The room was empty apart from Morgan and him, so he focused on Bennett's words.

"Which one?"

There was a hesitant pause on the other end of the line and he had to bite back a growl, wanting nothing more than to reach through the phone, grab Bennett and shake some answers out of him. He knew the answer though, in his heart of hearts. He just didn't want to admit it. Wanted to believe that his fated had stayed home tonight, washing her hair or something, and that Kait and Lilly were out with someone else.

"It's not…" He cleared his throat, meeting his demons head on with a calm, low voice. "Is it the Leroy girl?"

The next words out of Bennett's mouth shattered his hopes into a thousand pieces.

"Yeah, it's Kacie Leroy. How did you kn—"

The roar broke free before Dean could stop it; pain, fury and fear pouring straight from his heart and soul. Someone had hurt Kacie. Hurt his fated mate. His delicate, little *human* mate. His fragile little human mate.

Shit.

"Get it together, bro," he heard Morgan saying, the big warlock appearing a thousand miles away through the red-tinge over Dean's vision. "We can deal with this. You know we can."

He nodded and forced the primal rage pulsing from the feral parts of his soul down.

"Get her to the lodge," he ordered, his voice laden with the roughness of his bear trying to break free. All it wanted to do was tear through his human form and race to their mate's side. Protect her. Kill whoever had hurt her. Then Morgan could bring them back so he could kill the bastards again. And again. And again. Fuck, even centuries wouldn't be enough for him to slake the fury in his soul.

"Yes, Prime." Bennett's voice was level but wary. Dean recognized the tone. It was the sort people used when someone was on the edge and about to lose it totally. It was the same tone he'd been using with Kait Turner mere minutes ago.

"Now!"

"We're on our way," Bennett assured him. "Scott went to get a truck…" He paused for a second. "He's just about here now."

"Good. Don't waste time." With that last order, Dean cut the connection and looked up at Morgan. He knew his face was pale, the blood draining away in his shock.

"My mate's been hurt."

It was all he needed to say. All he *could* say. The thought of anything else was just too much to bear.

CHAPTER 2

*T*he truck pulled up outside the lodge in a screech of tires. Dean and Morgan were already moving before the vehicle had fully come to a stop. Yanking down the tailgate, Dean leaped up into the truck bed.

The first sight of Kacie, her normally golden skin pale and splattered with blood, several shirts wadded over her stomach, knocked all the breath out of him.

"Oh, sweetheart," he murmured, on his knees next to her as he reached out to brush her hair gently back from her face.

She lay so still. The dark eyes that usually spat fire and quick comments back at him were closed. He mourned their loss, wanting nothing more than to gather her into his arms as if he could make everything better by his touch alone. Hadn't alphas way back when been able to do that? Heal as well as fight? So the legends said anyway.

"Morgan…" He looked up at the other man in silent appeal. Dean was an alpha and a soldier. He knew about a hundred different ways to kill a man, but nothing about healing. Luckily, Morgan did.

"Let's see what we've got. *No, don't move her yet,*" the big warlock snapped when two of the younger bears in the truck started to pick up the body board Kacie had been strapped onto. His movements were efficient as he checked her over but, despite his calm expression and manner, Dean had seen enough wounded men to know the signs weren't good. She was too pale, her skin color was wrong and her breath came in short, sharp pants.

"Hold on there, babe," he whispered, unable to stop his fingertips brushing over her cheek. He'd never allowed himself to touch her before, so each stroke of her silken skin was precious.

"Okay, inside. Lift her carefully," Morgan ordered, his gaze snapping to Dean. "Your fated mate?"

There was a collective intake of breath, and all the bears in the truck tried their hardest not to have heard that little nugget of information. Dean sighed. There was no hiding it now even if he'd wanted to, so he nodded.

"She is."

"Good. Then I hope you're feeling strong, lover boy, because you're going to be using that bear of yours to power her healing."

"To my last breath," he promised, following the healer and his injured mate as she was carried inside.

Morgan took over, sweeping everything off the large dining table in the middle of Dean's quarters to clatter to the floor.

"On the table. Then get out," he ordered, already reaching inside his shirt for the leather bag around his neck as the bears rushed to do his bidding.

Dean blinked in surprise. Battered leather, Morgan had worn the small pouch around his neck for as long as Dean had known him, but he'd never actually seen the warlock open it.

He did now, chanting as he laid out the items within at intervals around Kacie's still form on the table. There was a small bundle of hair tied with a pink ribbon, a wolf's fang, a delicate gold earring, a small vial of something that shimmered gold and silver and, lastly, a man's silver ring.

As he placed the ring down, his blue eyes flicked up and speared Dean. "Shirt open."

"What? Didn't think you were inclined that way, bro," Dean chuckled, already ripping at the buttons to reveal a heavily muscled chest. Shit, Morgan could have told him to dance the fucking hula while wearing nothing but a pink tutu and a damn unicorn horn and he'd have done it. He'd do anything that would help his fated mate. Anything to have her up and about rather than motionless and pale on the table in front of him.

The ghost of a smile graced the other man's lips. "I'm not, not that it makes any difference. We're going to need skin-to-skin contact for this to work."

He moved forward, a small, very sharp knife suddenly appearing in his hand as he leaned over Kacie.

Dean snarled, the sound breaking free at the perceived threat to his mate. "What the fuck are you doing?"

The warlock didn't even look up. "Chill, big man. Skin to skin, remember? And the way your hands are shaking I don't want you anywhere near her with either a knife *or* claws."

He couldn't argue with that. Instead, he simply nodded as Morgan began to cut Kacie's top away with delicate movements, making sure to leave the makeshift dressing over her stomach in place. Dean couldn't even look at it. He knew exactly what damage claws could do to such soft, unprotected flesh. The thought of a bear doing that to her, to his little human, made him sick to his stomach. It fed the rage that tried to escape his control.

He refused to let it. Now was not the time or the place. First, he needed to make sure Kacie would live. His hands curled into hard fists, claws punching through his own skin and into his palms deeply enough for blood to run freely. But soon... soon he'd let the beast out on whoever had done this to her.

And they would pay. Dearly.

"Okay, we're good. On the table."

He didn't ask questions. Being careful not to jostle her, he climbed onto the table and reached out to pull Kacie into his arms. Even though she was unconscious, his body relaxed a fraction. Her weight against him felt right. She fit perfectly, like the other half of the puzzle that was him, her curves fitting against the harder planes of his body.

Closing his eyes, he buried his nose in her hair and took a deep breath.

"The first time I hold her," he admitted to

Morgan in a raw voice, "and she doesn't know a thing about it."

"Oh, she knows." The warlock moved around the table, his hands never ceasing in their movements as he drew symbols in the air. Dean couldn't see them, but then he didn't expect to. He never had, not in all their years of service. Apparently those without the sight couldn't see the magic...and shifter blood just wasn't magic enough. Practically boring according to the warlock. Dean had never known whether to be amused or insulted by that. He was a Prime, the most powerful bear in his clan and he was...not enough?

"She does?" he asked in surprise.

"Her breathing has calmed down and her heart rate has leveled out. Now will you stop fucking yapping so I can finish this spell and save your girlfriend?"

"Shutting up right now."

"Good." Morgan finished his circuit and came to stand by the side of the table. His expression was serious. "Right. I'm going to draw off some of the power of your bear to force her to heal. Humans really are rather simple to mend if you know what you're doing..."

Dean's lips didn't even quirk. "Can you quit fucking yapping and save my girlfriend?"

Morgan gave the tiniest grin, a twinkle in his eyes. "Yes, *Prime.* Might wanna brace yourself because this is probably going to hurt. A lot."

For the next hour Dean lay in silence, using his bigger body to cushion and cradle the silent woman in his arms. Morgan's spell snapped shut about them, an invisible cage the Prime felt pulling at him, trying to yank his bear's strength out through his very skin. It felt and sounded like they were in the center of a tornado, being buffeted and abused by the very air around them.

"Hold it. Control it!" Morgan roared over the chaos. "She can't take too much power at once… her body will burn out."

Dean nodded, sweat breaking out all over his skin as he forced his bear to remain in its cage, the door barely open to allow just enough power through. He didn't need Morgan's magical instincts to know that the spell had almost run its course. Make or break time.

Please Lady Luna, he sent a quick prayer up to the moon goddess he and some of his people still worshipped. *Let her live and I'm yours in this life and the next.*

Pain racked his body, from holding still for so long and from keeping the connection between him and his bear on a knife edge. But he was only a man, and his strength was finite.

"HOLD IT!" Morgan bellowed as he began to slip. Fear hit hard and fast then. He was too weak. He couldn't hold it. He would fail and Kacie would burn out... die.

Help came from an unexpected source. As he began to lose his grip on the connection between him and his beast, the bear didn't break free as he'd expected. Instead, the creature added its strength to his, supporting him as they both fed power to Kacie.

Ours. Protect. Heal, the beast rumbled.

Dean allowed himself a smile. *Yes. Ours.*

"That's it! It's working!" Morgan caroled in triumph, his voice raising to chant unintelligible words in a language Dean never wanted to hear ever again. They rose in a crescendo until...

Silence fell between one second and the next. Dean's breath rasped in his ears as he looked around, wondering if someone had let off a percussive grenade in the room and robbed him of hearing.

Morgan leaned over them, his fingers prying at the edges of the dressings across Kacie's midsection. They came away easily, the skin beneath unmarked.

"Holy shit," Dean breathed, hardly believing the evidence of his own eyes. Relief hit half a second later, making him shake and haul her closer in his hold. "It worked. It actually fucking worked!"

Morgan chuckled. "Of course it worked. What do you think I am, some kind of hedge-witch? Now, are you going to cuddle her all night or are you going to let me clean her up and check for any other wounds while you go and deal with whatever hell is breaking out with your bears in the other room?"

"Fuck."

At the warlock's words, Dean became aware of the growls and rumbles from the room next door. He wasn't sure how Primes from other clans handled things, but in the Beauty lodge, the Prime lived literally in the middle of things. His quarters were a two story apartment built right into the side of the bigger building. It meant that he was on hand to deal with most things that cropped up, which could be both a blessing and a curse.

It was a blessing when things like Kacie being injured happened and a curse when he wanted a bit of peace and quiet but kept getting interrupted by the werebear version of squabbling siblings.

Easing himself from his now peacefully sleeping mate, he slid off the table and stalked toward the door. He didn't care that his shirt was torn and covered in blood or that his bear had poked fur through his skin. After what he'd been through tonight, seeing his fated mate unconscious and bleeding from a gut wound inflicted by other bears, no one had better comment on his fashion sense. Not if they knew what was good for them.

He yanked the door open to find himself looking at a crowd. Well, the back of a crowd anyway. His eyes narrowed. What looked like most of the clan was packed into the main room of the lodge. He couldn't see to the commotion at the center of the room through the mass in front of him.

It was a large room, but the presence of so many bears made the air thick with shift potential, not to mention the threat of violence that was inherent anywhere large groups of bears gathered. Some of the males just couldn't keep their aggressive tendencies in check. Which was why the clan had enforcers—their very own police for want of a better word—responsible for ensuring the clan's laws were obeyed.

Like the two bears who were at the center of the commotion. Dean moved to the side to get a better view as a female voice cut through the noise of the crowd.

"Laws and regulations are what keep order. They protect not just our clan but all the clans. And there are consequences for breaking them."

Lilly Braun, his head enforcer, stood in the middle of the room, facing down another bear with a snarl on her lips and a furious expression. In the sudden silence the sound of her claws descending was a clear warning.

He craned his neck to see which asshole had pissed Braun off. An alpha female, she was more dangerous than most of the males in the clan and not a woman to tick off lightly. And from the look on her face, she was way past ticked off and heading into righteous fury territory.

The other bear had his back to Dean, but one look at the set of his shoulders and the back of his head made him hiss in recognition. Brad Harrison was one of the elitist pricks who'd been a pain in Dean's ass for the last couple of months.

The crowd murmured, the anticipation in the air matching that running through his veins. Perhaps he'd get lucky and Brad would piss Braun off enough that she'd kick his ass good and proper. He knew assholes like Brad through and through. The shame would be too much for him and he'd move on, becoming a problem for another Prime and another clan.

Or... he'd go rogue, like the ones who had attacked Kacie, Lilly and Kait, and become even more of a problem.

Another bear stepped forward, his big frame overshadowing Braun's as he took up position next to her. Brad's shoulders tensed as he looked up at the bigger man. Creed was another of the enforcer team, a man as big as a freaking bear and just as strong even in human form.

"I'm not breaking any laws," Brad whined, and then he seemed to shift tactic. "I challenge Creed for the right to claim the human woman."

Shit. That was what this was about. Instantly, Dean's eyes cut to Kait, half hidden behind Creed. She was pale, but that was no surprise. She'd just been thrust into what, for her, must be the stuff of nightmares and discovered that the bogeyman under the bed was, in fact, real.

"Creed?" Kait's expression was fearful. "Can he do that?"

"He can challenge." The big man's voice was a deep rumble, laden with his bear. One he didn't show often but that Dean knew was there. "But he has to meet me in the pit. And he's not fucking walking out of it alive."

His words broke the dam.

"Yeah? Says who, you fucking skin?" Brad surged forward, fury and violence written in every line of his body. "I'll tear you to fucking pieces and fuck your woman before your corpse is cold."

Dean bit back his chuckle. Brad was a relatively big bear when shifted, and pretty good with his claws, but Creed was something else entirely. He never fought shifted but he was lethal even in human form. Brad didn't stand a chance in the pit but was obviously too dumb to realize it.

"Just try it, asshole," Creed growled, stepping forward.

"Down boys," Lilly snapped, looking from one to the other. "Challenge has been called and accepted?"

At Creed's nod, she lifted her voice to address the room. "On behalf of Kaitlyn Turner, the challenged's mate, I claim rite of preparation. Challenge will be met in the pit in twenty-four hours."

"Hey, no!" Brad had been caught on the back foot and snarled in surprise. "She's not his mate, not yet. The rite of preparation doesn't apply."

Fuck's sake, Dean sighed. Some people would

argue anything, even set in stone laws like the rite. As the challenged, Creed was entitled to one full day with his woman, his mate, before he entered the pit to either live or die. It was one of their fundamental rights. And anyone who looked at the two, Kait's small hand on Creed's arm holding the big bear back even though he could easily have shrugged her off, could tell that if they weren't mated yet, they soon would be.

"In this case," Dean lifted his voice to carry over the room. The bears with their backs to him turned to look. "I rule that it does. Brad, if you have a problem with that, you can meet *me* in the pit now."

"No, Prime," Brad mumbled, dropping his gaze. "No problem at all."

"I didn't think so."

Dean transferred his attention to Creed and Kait. "Creed, take your woman home and prepare for the pit tomorrow."

"Prime." With a nod, Creed turned and, Kait's hand in his, left the lodge.

Dean stayed where he was, arms folded as he looked around the room. He'd have liked to say he was disappointed at how they'd come out of the woodwork at the possibility of fighting, but they were bears, violence was in their nature. It was unavoidable.

"Braun, Bennett... a word?" He stepped away from the door as the two walked over to him, the crowd dispersing at the same time. Some disappeared to rooms upstairs while others headed out the door presumably heading home. Only a few remained to nurse drinks and chat in small groups.

"Report," he ordered, looking at Braun first. She was the enforcer of the two, but Bennett's calm head in a bad situation hadn't escaped his notice.

"Five males, all bears, attacked us in the alley behind the library. It was obviously set up. They were waiting for us, some in front and some behind to cut off our escape." Anger flared in her eyes. "If I'd been on my own..."

He knew what she'd been about to say. If she'd been on her own and not worried about revealing what she was to two humans, she'd have torn through them. Sure, she might not have been able to take on five males by herself. Braun was as mean as they came in bear form, but even she wasn't *that* good, but she could certainly have held her own until help arrived.

"Shhh, don't worry about it," he said soothingly. "You did the right thing. Bennett?"

The younger bear shrugged. "Not much to tell, Prime. We were coming out of Beast when we caught the scent of unknown males. Then we heard the ruckus behind the library. By the time we got there it was all over and the attackers had gone. We'd have given chase, but Kacie..."

Dean's expression tightened and he held up his hand. "Again, you did the right thing. Any delay might have meant the death of a human—" And his mate, but he didn't add that. "—And, as you both know, the bear community as a whole can't afford that kind of scrutiny."

Both bears nodded in reply. The need to remain hidden was drilled into all of them as soon as they were old enough to realize they were different from other folks in town. It wasn't just Beauty either. There were other shifter clans nearby, and it wasn't unheard of for different shifter types to band together to wipe out any clan or pack who didn't play by the rules and advertised its presence to the humans around them.

"Braun, assemble the enforcers and send out recon teams. I want to know who these assholes are, their numbers and where they're holing up."

"Yes, Prime." Her reply was swift, rage still banked in her eyes.

"Do *not* engage," he ordered, knowing the she-bear would like nothing more than to storm into the rogue's camp and take them all apart piece by piece. "I want to know if they really are just a bunch of assholes acting alone or if there's another clan looking to move into our territory behind it."

Braun nodded. "On it, boss."

"Oh, and take Bennett. See if he's got the makings of an enforcer."

He hid his amusement as Braun huffed and shot the younger male a look.

"Come on then, and make sure to keep up or I swear I will cut your ass loose."

CHAPTER 3

*A*s a rule, Kacie Leroy never remembered her dreams.

So when she woke up, brain fuzzy with images of lying all warm and cozy in Dean Sterling's arms, she clung to the thoughts with everything she had, trying to grasp them before they disappeared under the brutal focus of full consciousness.

Keeping her eyes closed, she turned away from the light shining through her eyelids and willed herself to slide back into the wonderful dream. Well, she didn't really know whether it was a wonderful dream or not, but it had Dean in it, so it was already a hundred percent better than all the others. Of course, because this was Kacie and she'd always been a little aside from the norm, the dream also contained scary men with claws and, for some reason, her friend Lilly roaring like a bear and attacking people.

Wait…what? Delicate, I'll-cry-if-I-break-a-nail Lilly attacking people? She practically passed out if she got so much as a paper cut.

A snort of amusement brought Kacie the rest of the way out of sleep and the dream fragments scattered. She pouted, her eyes still closed. Well, wasn't that a total bunch of crapola? Best dream in a while and logic had to intrude to point out all the mistakes.

Like the fact that Dean Sterling would ever even *look* at her, never mind let her get all cozy and comfortable in his big, muscly arms. Oh well, a girl could dream, couldn't she? And she obviously had been.

Opening her eyes, she was preparing herself to haul up and out of bed when she stopped dead, eyes glued to the ceiling above.

The white plaster and beam ceiling most definitely wasn't hers.

Oh shit. Whose ceiling was that? Where the hell was she?

She snapped her eyes shut and squeezed them

tight to pray. *Please don't say I had a one night stand and called him Dean...*

"Oh, you're awake. Good," a deep male voice broke through her confusion, coming from somewhere behind her. With a start of surprise, she made to sit up and turn around but a hand landed on her shoulder. "No, don't move please. I want to make sure you're fully healed. And I need to give you something for the pain before you do."

"Healed? Pain?"

Kacie looked up in confusion as a tall man with sandy brown hair that flopped over blue eyes leaned over her. He looked familiar but she couldn't make her foggy brain figure out where she knew him from. It was only when he reached for her stomach that the spell broke.

"Hey, what the hell do you think you're doing?"

He paused, rocking back on his heels for a second to study her with an intent gaze. "You've been injured. You'll let me look at the site of the wound now."

She raised an eyebrow. With his firm, almost mesmerizing look and the deep, compelling tones of his voice, she could almost believe he was trying to brainwash her.

"Yeah, right. Who the hell are you anyway?"

"What?" The look of surprise that washed over his features almost made her snort with amusement. "No one's ever said no before. What do you mean, who am I? I'm Morgan Jones, I'm a he…" He paused, his expression altering just slightly. "I'm a doctor. I'm afraid you were involved in an accident, Miss Leroy. You're lucky to be alive."

Oh crap, an accident. That could explain a few things…

"Is that why my head is all fuzzy and I—"

She stopped talking, aware she'd been about to admit to having what amounted to wet dreams about Dean, and suddenly remembered where she knew him and his name from.

"Morgan Jones? Dean Sterling's army buddy?"

He favored her with a quick smile as he shone a small pen light in her eyes, one after the other. "That's right. We served in the same unit for a few years."

Kacie relaxed. Now she remembered seeing him with Dean in the Beast Bar a few times, his tall, broad-shouldered physique and handsome face setting all the local single ladies atwitter. Not her though. Morgan was handsome and everything, but she'd always had a thing for hot ex-jock soldiers like Dean.

"Okay." She nodded to give him permission, watching the ceiling as he peeled away the covers over her stomach. "Was it a bad accident?"

"Uh-huh, really quite nasty. Fortunately, we got to you in time." He made a pleased sound and pressed the dressing back down over her stomach. "It's all looking good. It might pull a little at first but then it should ease up."

"Thanks, I'll be careful. Am I okay to shower or get it wet?"

He nodded. "Sure. You can actually remove the dressing if you want the next time you do. Just be careful, these army ones... they like to hang on to some skin when you take them off. Get it wet and peel slowly. Don't pull, okay?"

"Got it, Doc. Thanks."

"You can sit up now. *Slowly*," he warned, watching her carefully as she levered herself up into a sitting position.

Her head swam a little but quickly eased up. However, the rest of her felt somewhat odd. She felt energized. Almost like she'd stuck her finger in a wall socket to charge but without the unfortunate side effects of frizzy hair or dying.

She took a look around the room. She'd expected

comfortable hospital surroundings but it appeared to be some kind of lounge…

"Why am I on the table?"

"It was the quickest place to bring you for treatment." Morgan shrugged as she swung her legs over the edge of the table. As he'd warned, her stomach pulled like she'd done a thousand sit-ups and she tensed. But the feeling faded and she carried on the rest of the way.

"Really?" Alarm bells began to ring in Kacie's head. From the way he'd been talking, she'd been moments away from death, so they brought her to… she took a better look at the room around her… some kind of hunting lodge?

Sliding off the table, she backed up a couple of steps and fixed the doctor, if he even was one, with a firm look. "Okay, mister, you'd better tell me exactly what the hell is going on here."

"I think that's where I need to tap out." Morgan looked over her shoulder as the door opened behind her. "You can explain this shit-storm to her, not me."

"What shit-storm?" She whirled around to find Dean framed in the doorway. The sight of him took her breath away, but she was used to it, concealing her intake of breath with a scowl. "What are you doing here?"

"Maybe because I live here?" He nodded to Morgan as the tall doctor left the room, shutting the door behind him. She got a brief glimpse of another room but couldn't make out any details before her view was cut off.

"If I was in an accident, why was I brought here rather than taken to a hospital?" Folding her arms defensively over her chest, she waited for his answer.

The pause before he answered gave other questions time to crowd through her brain. Like had he seen her when she was asleep? Oh my god, had she drooled? *Please tell me I didn't drool. Not in front of Dean Sterling.* That was so not sexy. Looking down at herself, she frowned.

She wore her going out jeans, the ones so tight they were practically sprayed on, paired with a large white t-shirt that wasn't hers. Easy to tell because it buried her and she preferred her t-shirts fitted and lower cut. Girl had a figure, she had to show it off, that was the law... but if she had her going out stuff on...

"Oh shit." Her eyes widened as she looked up at him. The next second she hurried around the table, searching under it and around the chairs for her purse. "What time is it? And where's my cell? Kait and Lilly will be so worried!"

"Hey, hey... calm down." Somehow Dean had crossed the room without her realizing, taking her into his arms as her head swam with her sudden movement. She clung to him, wrapping her hands around the big, muscular upper arms she'd been dying to touch for years. "You were badly injured. You need to take it easy."

His touch and the very real experience of being in Dean Sterling's, the guy she'd had a crush on since she was in pigtails, arms was enough to short-circuit her brain for a second. Her response was to look up into his handsome face with a dumbfounded, "Huh?"

She closed her eyes for a second. *Smooth, Kacie, real smooth. He probably thinks you're a sandwich short of a freaking picnic now.*

"Kacie? Sweetheart, open your eyes."

Shaking her head, she kept them shut.

"No. Won't."

This was so not happening. Dean was not holding her close and cozy-like, and he had no way just called her sweetheart. That last bit sealed the deal. She was still dreaming. That's why nothing made sense. That's why she was in Dean's arms and he'd just called her sweetheart in that soft, sexy voice she'd imagined so many times in her dreams.

His chuckle was deep and masculine, sending a shiver down her spine. "Why not?"

She bit her lip as he touched her, brushing a strand of hair behind her ear. It was such a cliché move, she knew that, but her knees didn't care and weakened instantly. Damn traitors.

"Because this is such a nice dream, and if I do, it'll all be over and I won't remember it." Oh great, now her mouth was operating without the intervention of her brain. Because she hadn't, like, wanted to keep any of her dignity. Pffft, who needed the stuff anyway?

"Okay."

He didn't argue with her about it just being a dream. Figured. Even her imaginary Dean knew this would so not be happening in real life. No matter how she felt about the handsome ex-jock turned soldier, no matter how many covert glances she'd stolen in Beasts, he had never once looked at her in *that* way.

"Okay?" she frowned, eyes still shut. Apparently a girl did have some pride after all…

"Because with your eyes closed, you can't stop me doing this."

Her eyes flew open as the words were whispered against her lips, only to flutter closed again with a soft moan as his mouth claimed hers. His lips were warm and firm, brushing against hers lightly. Softly, like he didn't want to scare her off.

She almost laughed at the thought. He should think himself lucky she didn't hook her leg behind his, throw him to the floor and pin him down to ravish him. Yeah, right... like she would *ever* do that. She was more likely to freak out and run. Only the fact that this was fantasy rather than reality kept her where she was. Because it *was* a dream, she could enjoy it and not worry about what people thought.

"Don't stop," she begged when he lifted his head. She opened her eyes to find him watching her, a strange look in his eyes. "I like it when you kiss me."

"Moon's balls, Kacie," he groaned, one hand coming up to slide into her hair and hold her still. "You'll be the death of me. You have no idea how long I've wanted to do this."

She couldn't answer, didn't get time anyway as his lips crashed down over hers. This time he wasn't soft or gentle. His mouth claimed hers in a hard, passionate kiss that shattered what defenses she had left against him to smithereens.

He explored her lips, learning their shape and texture, and then parted them with a hard sweep of his tongue. She opened for him with a soft murmur, hands bunched in the fabric of his shirt, and he pushed inside. He explored the soft recesses of her mouth with devastating finesse. His tongue found hers and coiled around it, stroking and sliding.

She gasped, the sound lost under his lips, and kissed him back. She'd never been a pliant or passive woman, not generally and definitely not when it came to the bedroom. She knew what she liked, what she wanted, and she wasn't shy about getting it.

Easing closer, she wound her arms around his neck and kissed him back. She matched each of his strokes and slides with one of her own, forcing the tension and awareness between them higher rapidly.

Her fingers found the short hairs at the back of his head, stroking through them. Being kissed by Dean was like nothing she'd ever imagined—and she'd thought about it a lot. He was hard and forceful, but not rough or harsh. She could spend an eternity in his arms and consider herself a happy woman.

She pouted when he pulled back, gentling her with softer kisses until he broke away to look down at her. His breathing was ragged and his eyes dark with heat. A heat so dark and dangerous that her body clenched in response.

"Slow," he muttered, as though to himself. "I promised I'd go slow. Be careful."

"Promised who?" She reached up to trace her finger over the full curve of his lower lip. "There's only the two of us here and I didn't make *any* promise to behave..."

The growl was lower this time and whispered over her skin. It was such a deep and primal sound that she paused, looking around the room to make sure no dangerous animal had gotten in with them. But it hadn't. Her eyes widened. No, the sound had definitely come from Dean.

"Fucking hell, Kacie... you have no idea what you're saying, what you're doing to me..." Expression tortured, he leaned down to press his forehead against hers.

"Just kiss me again," she whispered, not understanding the problem. It figured even her dream version of Dean would be reluctant. "What's so wrong with that?"

"This," he snarled, grabbing her hand and shoving it down to his groin. She gasped as his cock pressed into her palm, as thick and rigid as a steel pole. "And because I don't think I'll be able to stop."

"Oh." She couldn't think of anything else to say,

swaying on her feet as he put her from him suddenly.

His hazel gaze searched her face. "There's lots you need to know, but not now. You're tired, and you've been injured. Sleep, heal… and then we'll talk."

"Talk now," she demanded mulishly, folding her arms. But as though mention of the word had summoned it, a wide yawn washed over her and exhaustion rose up to rob her of strength. Could she be tired *in* a dream? That seemed odd but she let the thought go in favor of meeting his gaze with a firm one of her own. "Okay, tomorrow, but you need to tell me everything. Deal?"

"Deal," he nodded, watching her strangely as she yawned again. "Now let's get you settled in the spare room."

Kacie Leroy would be the death of him. Either with her kisses, or when she found out that he'd lied to her for years.

Was still lying to her…

But how was he going to tell her the truth?

Hey, Kacie. You know those films about monsters and

werewolves? Yeah, well... I'm a werebear. Which is like a werewolf... but a bear. And I live outta town in a den with lots of others who get furry a couple of times a month.

Yeah, like that was going to go down well. He could imagine the response. She'd think he was a complete and utter lunatic and drive him straight to the nearest mental health unit.

Unless he changed in front of her...

Which, if she took it badly, meant *he* could be driving *her* to the mental health unit.

Dean sighed as he sat in the Prime's large, carved chair in its place of honor next to the clan's pit. Easily thirty feet across, it was exactly what the name suggested—a large hole in the ground, the earth around it shored up with wooden planks. They were scarred with claw marks from years of challenges.

It wasn't empty. Two bears stood facing each other on the packed earth, anger written on their faces as the edges of the pit filled with clan bears eager to see the outcome of the match.

He flicked a glance around the assembled faces. All the clan were here, apart from those too young to know what was going on, and Elisa Watson, who'd just had a baby. Unlike some Primes (his own father for one), Dean had never been a hardass about clan members being present at all challenges.

His expression tightened a fraction as he noted a small knot of people about a third of the way around the pit wall from him. His bear growled as he recognized Anderson and his cronies.

"Sure you want to do this, skin?" Harrison taunted Creed as the two men circled each other. Creed was the larger of the two, but despite the fact he was one of Dean's enforcers, most of the clan looked down on him because he didn't shift. Ever.

The guy *was* a shifter, that was for sure. His scent reeked of bear, but even Dean had only ever seen him shift a couple of times, and certainly not with the ease the rest of them could. He'd asked Creed about it, but all the big man would say was that it was like being skinned alive with knives of fire. As an alpha, Dean could force him to shift if he needed to, but knowing it caused his friend pain had always stayed his hand.

Besides, Creed was a mean son of a bitch at the best of times and could fight just as easily, and lethally, in human form. Not many bears developed that skill. They didn't need to with their shift ability. So a shifter who could fight human? They bore watching.

After dancing around for a while, Harrison finally got his act together and threw a punch. Creed just looked bored, watching the jab as it sailed through the air and then sliding to the side just before it hit.

The crowd gathered around the edges of the pit oohing and awwwing at the display of speed. Anticipation and eagerness thickened in the air as they jostled each other for a better view.

"Come on, skin..." Harrison taunted as he kept up the jabs, obviously not intelligent enough to realize that his opponent avoiding or blocking his blows was not his opponent going on the offensive.

Creed circled him around the pit, throwing the occasional punch that Harrison easily shrugged off. Creed was testing the younger man's reactions and defenses but again, Harrison didn't appear to realize that and crowed with triumph every time he blocked his opponent's blows.

"What's the matter with you?" he sneered. "Scared to fight me?"

Creed didn't answer, his guard up as he rolled his shoulders like a boxer. Dean merely sat back in his chair, his comfortable lounge belying his interest. He'd seen Creed fight before. When he clicked his shoulder, shit was about to get real.

Harrison laughed as he dropped his guard, obviously buying into all the rumors that had been floating around the clan for years about Creed. That he was a half-skin, a human with a little bit of bear blood but not a real bear. Not a real threat. The laugh turned into a roar as he changed, his bear unfolding from his human form almost lazily.

Had he been any other bear, Dean would have suspected he'd changed slowly on purpose. To prove he could do it and as a subtle snub to Creed that he wasn't a dangerous enough opponent to warrant a fast change. But no, as Prime he knew the capabilities of all his bears and Brad Harrison really was a slow shifter.

Harrison, now fully furred up, roared across the pit. Creed ignored him, lifting his hand to study his fingernails as though checking whether they were dirty or not.

The fact his opponent didn't consider him a threat seemed to piss Harrison right off. Dropping to all fours, he charged. The crowd held their breath. With the big bear lumbering toward him, Creed's admittedly big frame seemed dangerously small and fragile. He'd be torn apart by Harrison's lethally sharp claws...

Just before the bear reached him, Creed looked

up, yawned and twisted to the side. Almost bending over backward, he slid under Harrison's paw and front leg as he lashed out with his claws. They slashed across the air where Creed's head had been moments before, hitting the side of the pit and biting deeply into the wood.

The bear grunted in surprise, the sound carrying across the pit, but before he could yank his claws free, Creed had moved. Lightning fast, he hammered three or four blows into the bear's furry side. When the last blow hit, Creed's knuckles buried in Harrison's fur, bone cracked like a gunshot. A broken rib... a favorite move of Creed's. Dean was surprised Harrison had fallen for it. Surely he'd asked people about how Creed fought before facing him in the pit?

The bear grunted in pain, wheeling away to favor that side as he tried to track his opponent around the pit. Creed didn't give him a chance to settle down or catch his breath though. Throwing dirt up into Harrison's eyes, he attacked hard and fast, stepping in close to Harrison to slam blow after blow into his furry opponent.

He danced around the bear, making Harrison howl in pain and fury as he twisted and turned, trying to land a claw on the still human Creed. But he was too fast, never where Harrison thought he was going to be, or already moved on from where he had been. He added slaps in between the punches, enraging Harrison and making him lose his temper.

Not for long though. A right hook to the jaw threw Harrison's head to the side with a meaty crack. A tooth flew loose from the bear's mouth, embedding itself in the wood like a bullet as blood splattered around it.

The bear staggered to the side, shaking his head. Then his back legs folded under him and he sat down heavily, an almost comical look of surprise on his furry face. It seemed a world where he didn't win hadn't occurred to him.

Dean rose to his feet, his expression set as he looked down into the pit. Harrison was still sitting, but had started to sway from side to side as though he were in his own private little world.

So be it.

They'd all known the outcome of this match before it had begun. Only idiots like Harrison with his puppet master, Anderson, whispering sweet nothings in his ear, thought otherwise.

"Since Harrison looks to be unable to continue the fight," Dean announced, pitching his voice to carry to all those crowded around the pit, "I declare Creed the winner."

A cheer went up from the crowd, proving again just how well-liked Creed was, despite his reticent bear. Only Anderson's little group turned away, muttering angrily among themselves. Dean sighed. There was a problem he was going to have to sort out, and soon. Because he'd turned to watch them go, he missed movement in the pit below.

"No! Creed, watch out!" Kait's scream made him snap his head around to see Harrison surge forward and swipe his claws across Creed's unprotected back. Creed staggered, his face suddenly pale. Several bears lifted their heads and sniffed as a metallic scent hit the air.

"The bastard used Carve!" Lilly roared as she dropped into the pit at the same time.

"You want to poison someone, asshole?" Lilly snarled, backing Harrison up into the corner. "How about you try that on me?"

"And me," Dean snarled, dropping down into the pit next to her. Other bears lined the edge of the pit, ready to help but none dared drop down with both Lilly and Dean in there.

He didn't expect them to. *No one* in their right mind wanted to get into the pit with him, not for any reason. Not when he loosed his hold on his bear and let the beast start to broaden his back. The two of them stood between Harrison and Creed, shielding the stricken bear as they advanced on his attacker.

Fury swirled through Dean. To attack a man when his back was turned was the lowest form of cowardice—something he didn't like to see from any bear in his clan.

"See? *See!* It wasn't Carve!" Harrison all but screamed, sweating where he was pinned between Lilly and Dean, and pointing toward Creed. "How could he be on his feet if it was Carve? He'd be deader than a dodo!"

Dean looked over his shoulder to see Creed roll to his feet.

"He's mine," the big man growled.

The murderous expression warned Dean to move out of the way and fast. He might be Prime and mean as fuck in a fight, but there were some looks in a man's eye that warned a brother not to fuck with him. Harrison had put a claim in for Creed's woman and then tried to kill the man himself—and not in a fair fight. It would be fair to say that Creed was pissed, and from the look on his face, hell was coming with him.

Dean shrugged and stepped back, spreading his arms. "He attacked while your back was turned. He's all yours."

He turned away. Lilly followed him, pausing for a moment to murmur to Harrison, "May your soul be welcomed with loving arms."

It was the bear prayer, said to those who were certain to die. The last rites of the furry kind. It was all they said, all they needed.

"What?" Fear filled Harrison's voice as the two walked away, leaving him with Creed. Dean reached Kait, cupping his hands to boost her up out of the pit before hauling himself out with a swift move that spoke of long experience.

"No, no, no..." Harrison whined. "You can't leave me with him. It wasn't Carvix. It was horse sedative mixed with rat poison. Just something to slow him down."

"Makes no difference," Creed growled and then grinned. Even Dean would have given it up as a bad job and hauled ass out of the pit if he'd seen that expression on an opponent. "You've had your fun. Now it's my turn."

Then Creed...changed faster than any bear Dean had ever seen. Apart from himself, of course. Within a heartbeat, his tall figure was replaced by four hundred pounds of pissed-off werebear.

"Please, no, don't hurt me…" Brad whimpered.

From then on, the fight went quickly. Dean stood by, next to Kait, in case she needed anything. Most of his attention was on the fight though. For all that Creed was one of his, he'd be failing in his duty as Prime if he didn't study how all his bears fought. One day he could be facing a challenge from any of them.

He sure hoped it wasn't Creed. As a man, he was dangerous, but as a bear…

"Fuck me," Lilly whispered. "He's freaking lethal."

"Agreed," Dean murmured. "Not on the fucking thing though. No offense."

"None taken," the she-bear replied, folding her arms as Creed finished the fight right there in front of them.

Standing, Creed folded his bear back inside and growled at his whimpering and bleeding opponent. "Fuck off, Harrison, and remember today. Remember you owe me your life."

The beaten bear scuttled off as fast as his legs could carry him.

"Anyone else?" Creed challenged the crowd clustered around the pit. There was a shuffling of feet and a general avoidance of his gaze as no one answered. Dean hid his smirk. Yeah, right. After seeing Creed in action, none of them wanted to step in the pit with him, and Dean didn't blame them.

"That's it, folks. Show's over." He stepped forward, drawing all eyes to him. "That means buggar off and go home!"

CHAPTER 4

*T*he next time Kacie woke, she was alone and her head was a lot clearer. For a moment she lay there, looking up at yet another ceiling that wasn't hers. Then her memory kicked in.

"Oh. Oh, *shit.*"

Heat flooded her cheeks as she remembered being in Dean's arms, being kissed... Oh god, that had really happened, hadn't it? She pressed her hands to her cheeks in an attempt to cool them down, a small squeak of dismay escaping her lips. Shit, shit, *shit.* She'd thought she was in a dream, but she must just have been rattled from the accident.

She stopped, hands halfway down from her face. Her mind filled with memories of the alley, big men attacking, the flash of claws in the moonlight. Pain in her stomach and blood everywhere. Then…nothing.

"Oh my god…" she breathed, horrified. They'd been attacked behind the library. How the *hell* could she have forgotten? Horror filled her. Shit, were Kait and Lilly okay? Of the three of them she was the most capable, the other two wouldn't have stood a chance.

"Dean! *Dean!*" she bellowed, hurtling herself out of bed and across the room like a small, human-shaped missile.

Reaching the door, she almost yanked it off its hinges and raced through it. The unfamiliar corridor took her aback for a moment. She'd never been in Dean's house. Hell, before now she'd hardly been on speaking terms with the guy. Ogling, yes. Speaking, no. Apparently though, if her memories were correct, they'd skipped speaking and gone right the way up to near-sex-while-standing terms.

"Dean!" she yelled again, trying each door in the corridor as she passed it. For heaven's sakes, how many rooms did one guy need? Had he gone out?

She got her answer as the last door opened before she touched the handle, revealing Dean, naked to the waist with rumpled bedhead.

Ohmyfuckinggodhesgorgeous.

She stopped dead, like a rabbit caught in the headlights, her eyes wide and riveted to the wide expanse of chest with its sexy smattering of hair.

"You yelled? Is everything okay?" he asked, his voice all sexy and deep from sleep. Within a few seconds, though, his gaze sharpened and became worried. Instantly, he was by her side, taking her hand in his as his free arm wrapped around her waist like he was worried she'd collapse right there on the landing.

"Uh, yeah. I'm fine," she answered automatically and then quickly gathered her wits about her.

"We were attacked. By men with..." Oh fucking hell, he was going to think she was crazy. "With knives. Are Kait and Lilly okay? Please tell me someone's checked on them."

"Knives, huh?" He had an odd look on his face as he led her into the room, the door swinging shut behind them. She tried to ignore the fact that it was his bedroom, and the big, wide bed was the one he'd just slept in. "Are you sure it was knives?"

No, it was goddamn claws, but she couldn't tell him that. She nodded. "Uh-huh, definitely knives. One of them..."

She trailed off, her hand smoothing over her

stomach. A frown creased her brow as she tried to make all the pieces of her memory fit. "One of them stabbed me. That's why there was so much blood. But for an abdominal wound…"

Her words trailed off again and she just looked at him. Nothing at all about this situation added up, and she couldn't blame it on a dream or the after effects of an accident now. Which left either the possibility that she'd fallen down some freakishly big rabbit hole, or she didn't have all the information she needed. But Dean obviously did…

"Right, handsome. How about you start telling me the truth?" she said, scooting away from him on the bed. Not far, just enough to put a little distance between them so she could collect herself.

She had to be realistic. Dean was a big man, and fast as hell… or he used to be at school. Like the rest of the girls, she'd watched him on the field and boy, the guy could *move.* She didn't suppose his service in the army had lessened that speed, probably increased it, what with people shooting at him and all. So, if he wanted to grab her, there wasn't much she could do about it.

"I don't know what you mean." He gave her that little half-smile and confused shake of the head that all but short-circuited her brain. But she was onto him now. Either he was the world's biggest cute but gullible nice guy, or he was playing her with misdirection and her own feminine responses.

"I'll lay it out for you then, shall I, hotshot?" she cut in, anger and frustration making her voice rise.

"We were attacked by men with knives. I'll call them knives, but right now? I'm not convinced they weren't something else. No," she snapped, lifting a finger when he opened his mouth to speak. "You don't get to talk yet. I am. So... we were attacked and I was stabbed in the stomach. Now, since you're a veteran, I'm assuming you've done more than basic level first aid. So you know that the appropriate emergency treatment for abdominal wounds is to take the casualty to a hospital... *NOT* the dining room of whatever guy finds them, no matter how sexy he is. So, cut me a break and tell me what the hell is actually going on here?"

He considered her for a long moment, and then slowly, a broad grin spread over his face. "So you think I'm sexy?"

THE LOOK that flashed across Kacie's beautiful heart-shaped face was a mix between frustration and rage, tempered with a little, more than a little, feminine interest. Whatever it was, Dean found it utterly fascinating and delightful.

"Anyone ever tell you that you're cute when you're mad?" he murmured, reaching forward to chuck her under the chin.

Anger flared in her eyes and she shook off his touch. "Only those with a frigging death wish. Now are you going to explain why you didn't take me to a hospital and..." Her face fell. "Oh god, Lilly's terrible with blood, she'd have passed out. Kait's made of stronger stuff so she'd probably be alright. *Please,* are my friends okay?"

The pleading note and the way she looked at him, like he could make everything in her world okay again, did him. That trust humbled him. Scooting closer to her on the bed, he took her hand in his.

"I promise. Your friends are fine. Lilly didn't pass out—" He had to smother his smile at the idea of the head enforcer being squeamish about blood. She wasn't, no alpha could be in a clan structure, but he understood why she'd let her human friends think that. "— And Kait is definitely made of stronger stuff." Strong enough to accept that her soul mate was a bear-shifter anyway.

Before answering her other questions, he closed his eyes for a second, preparing himself. He had to get this right. Not just almost right, or nearly right, but spot-on, one hundred percent *dead* right. Bear clans didn't have many when it came to laws, so the ones they did have were cast in stone. The most sacred of those was that humans did not know about bears.

If they found out, one of two things happened. They either mated a bear... or they were killed. No ifs, buts or maybes about it. Dead.

But he couldn't kill Kacie. That knowledge welled up from the center of his soul and he knew he just couldn't do it. He couldn't even give the order to someone who could. If she rejected him as a mate...

He opened his eyes and looked up, studying the ceiling without seeing it. He'd send her away, say she had mated someone else. It would kill him but, hell, he'd even find her a suitable mate himself. Anything as long as she lived. *Anything.*

A soft touch on his arm brought him back to the present, and he looked down into her chocolate-colored eyes.

"Still with me?" she asked in a soft voice. "You went somewhere else there for a moment."

She grounded him. Completed him. Dean sighed. And he had to tear her understanding of the world apart.

"We didn't take you to a human hospital because they couldn't have treated you." In the end he went for bluntness and honesty. "The men who attacked you weren't men. They weren't human and those weren't knives they were carrying."

She nodded slowly, keeping her gaze on his. He could see the cogs turning behind her eyes and pride filled him. His mate was smart. She'd already started to put it together even though it didn't make any sense to her.

"They were—"

"Claws," she cut in. "They were claws. And if they were claws, they could have given me something, couldn't they? Like rabies?"

He managed a small nod. "Possibly."

"So what were they? You said they weren't men."

"They were ursanthropes."

"Ursanthropes?" Her brow furrowed at the unfamiliar word. "What, like lycanthropes?"

"The same thing, yes, but lycanthropes are wolves. Ursanthropes are bears. Bear-shifters to be precise."

"Bears."

Just one word. That's all she said, watching him like he'd gone out of his mind. He braced himself, waiting for either hysterics or outright laughter. Neither seemed immediately forthcoming. Instead, she sat next to him on the bed in silence, a thoughtful look on her face.

Dean held his breath, hardly daring to hope. His bear was equally quiet, as though it too, held its breath waiting for her answer.

Finally, she looked up at him, curiously. "I take it you're one…a bear?"

"Yes, sweetheart. I am."

Just that little admission felt good down to his soul. He'd told his fated mate what he was. Now all that remained was to show her and then bite her… He hauled his over-active imagination back from its little joyride. She had to actually say yes to being his mate first…

He didn't stop her as she reached out, touching his chest lightly. He flexed his pec just as she did, making her jump and squeak.

"Dean Sterling!" she gasped, slapping his arm lightly. "Stop making me jump."

"I won't do it if you touch me again," he

promised, and he didn't. He just watched as she reached out to press her fingertips lightly against his skin.

"Your bear is inside you?" She seemed fascinated, but he wasn't complaining. Being touched by her, the feel of her soft little hands smoothing over his chest was like all his Christmases come at once.

"Yeah…" His voice was a little deeper than usual but not because of his bear. That was a purely human male reaction to her touch and events south of the border. With her hands on him and her scent in the air, he was already at half-mast and praying like hell she didn't look down at his lap. "You want to meet him?"

Her eyes flicked to his. "It's a he? Does he have a name?"

Amusement bubbled over, and Dean barked out a short laugh before he could stop himself. "Of course it's a he. I'm male, which means he is. And no, bears don't really have names in that way. He's alpha, he's Prime… that's all he needs."

"You're an alpha… like an alpha male?"

The way she flicked her small pink tongue over her lower lip to wet it made him bite back a groan, but it was the sudden scent of her interest and arousal in the air that really tested his control. His bear roared at him, demanding to know why they weren't claiming their mate when she was...Right. Freaking. There.

"Oh, yeah... I'm all alpha, sweetheart." *Oh god, touch me again. Lower, that's it... down the abs...* His inner demon started up the monologue as Kacie's hands began to wander. Before she slid down too far though, he caught her wrists. "And if you carry on like that, baby, you're gonna find out *exactly* how much."

"Oh, really?" Her eyebrow winged up but she didn't try and release her wrists from his grasp. Instead she flexed her hand, managing to reach far enough to stroke his skin with her fingertips. "Shouldn't tease a gal with promises like that."

Holy. Shit. He'd just told her he was a werebear, and that... and she...

Adjusting his position so she couldn't touch him, he warned her again. "Kacie, stop it. I'm not playing games now. If you carry on I *will* pin you to this bed, and I won't let you up until you're mine in every sense of the word."

"Please."

The soft word and the look in her eyes pole-axed him. It couldn't be this easy, surely? He searched her eyes, checking for any tell-tale signs of mania or other indicators of hysteria. Her lips curved in a fond smile, and instantly he felt like he was missing something.

"Dean, I've known there's something odd about this town for years. The way half of you disappear around the full moon or rush off en-masse randomly? It's kind of a dead giveaway. And…" The smile became a full-blown grin. "At least you're not aliens. *That* would have been just weird. Bears?" She shrugged. "There have always been bears around here. At least now I know that not all of them are sizing me up for a quick snack."

He yanked her closer, tumbling her into his lap. "Oh, I plan on eating you alright, sweetheart, but it won't be a snack…more an all you can eat buffet and I won't stop until you're hoarse from screaming my name."

With that, he slid a hand into her hair, and, confident of his reception, bent his head to claim her lips.

She opened for him immediately, granting him access to the soft, warm secrets of her mouth. He groaned as he pushed in, finding her tongue with his. She was soft, sweet and oh-so-addictive. And she was all his… Finally his.

The groan became a growl as he lifted her,

settling her down so she straddled his lap. She wore one of his t-shirts, the fabric sliding up her curvy thighs as she lowered herself. He swallowed her little gasp as she felt his cock for the first time—hard and heavy where it pressed into the groove of her pussy lips. He couldn't resist a small rock of his hips. The movement, the friction, made them both gasp.

He did it again, feeling damp heat through the thin layers that separated them. Layers he wanted to rip away so he could bury himself balls deep in her tight pussy. She would feel like heaven. He just knew she would.

"Oh... that feels good," she whispered as she rocked her hips in time with his. The feel of her moving against him almost unmanned him there and then. He'd not been so close to coming in his shorts in years. Not since he was a gangly teenager who'd yet to learn control.

"Real good, and it's about to feel a whole lot better," he promised, dropping back to lie on his back on the bed and looking up at her. Color flushed her cheeks, her dark hair a messy cloud around her face, and her lips betrayed the fact she'd been thoroughly kissed. In short, she looked like she'd just rolled out of bed... with him.

And it looked good on her.

He drank in the sight of her there, straddling his lap, and slid his hands up the sides of her thighs. One hand on his stomach for balance, her eyelids fluttered shut, a soft sound of pleasure escaping her lips.

He reached the hem of the t-shirt and slid his hands under, the white fabric bunched on his wrists as he explored her skin beneath. Her breathing hitched, breasts moving under the thin fabric with each inhalation. She wasn't wearing a bra, her tight nipples tempting him as they poked stiffly against the fabric.

His fingertips found the edges of her panties and he groaned. The strap was the thinnest thing, barely there. Too narrow for anything but...

"A thong. You're determined to kill me, aren't you?"

He barely recognized his voice, the deep growl thick with lust and dirty thoughts.

She opened her eyes and shrugged, a look of pure mischief flitting across her face. "Easy access... you just gotta slide them to the side."

Fuck. Me.

As though her words were a command, he traced the line of her panties down and between her legs. She bit her lip as the broad, blunt edges of his fingers brushed against her satin-covered pussy lips. A tiny rock of her hips urged him on. Hand shaking, he dipped a finger beneath the fabric and swept it through her lower lips. Slick heat welcomed him, her soft moan a treasure he locked away tight in his memory for all time.

"So wet," he murmured, pushing the scrap of satin out of the way to stroke again. Easily he found her clit, smoothing the slickness of her arousal over and around the tiny bundle. She whimpered, her eyes closed as she rocked against his hand.

He pleasured her, teasing her clit with hard strokes and then soft circles. Never enough for her to latch onto a rhythm, but each move designed to feed the fire inside her body. His own roared and demanded he shove his pajama pants down and fill her with his cock, but he held off. He wanted...no, he *needed* to do this. He needed her to come apart in his arms, screaming his name as he made her come.

"Oh god, Dean. More... please, more."

She was so responsive he couldn't help wanting to give her everything. Moving without warning, he flipped them over until she was on her back in the middle of the bed. Her squeak was a surprised one that rolled into a moan when he pushed her legs farther apart.

"You wanted more. More you get," he breathed against her inner thigh. Her whole body tensed as he kissed his way up toward her pussy. With gentle fingers he pulled her panties aside and lowered his head. He gave her a long lick from her slit right up to her clit.

Her taste, musky and sweet and perfect, exploded on his tongue and he felt his control slipping. He'd been planning to stop at just making her come but once he'd tasted her... all bets were off now. When he was done eating her out and making her scream, he was going to turn her over, pull her ass up into the air and bury himself balls deep in her tight little pussy.

"Oh... *Ohhhh...*"

That's it, sweetheart, just like that. Sliding his hand up her thigh, he teased the entrance to her body with his fingers, easing the tip of one digit just into her channel and then pulling out again. She gasped, rocking against him in a silent plea for more.

Rap-rap-rap.

They both froze at the knock on the door. Dean didn't move, swirling his tongue over her clit in a way that made her wriggle and whimper. Whoever it was could just fuck off. He had better things to do.

Like screw the living daylights out of his little human mate.

"Prime?" It was Bennett's voice. "Sorry to bother you when you're... busy, but we have a problem in the office."

Dean lifted his head. With a bear's sense of smell, there was no way Bennett didn't know what they were up to. "Can't it wait?"

"Sorry, Prime. It's Anderson."

He didn't need to say anymore. Dean sighed. The sheriff was a recurring pain in the ass, turning up in his office at least once a week to rant about something or other.

"Okay, give me a minute. I'll be right down."

"As you will, Prime."

As Bennett's footsteps faded down the corridor, Dean gave Kacie's clit one last little lick and then crawled up to brace himself over her. She looked so sexy, her eyes dark with need and her cheeks so flushed that he almost gave in to the temptation to drop his pants and take her right then. But a quick, dirty fuck was not the way he wanted to take his fated for the first time.

"I have to deal with this," he whispered, by way of apology.

"Bear stuff?" she whispered back, even though

they were the only two in the room and there was no need for silence. It was nice. It felt conspiratorial.

"Well," she said with a sexy drawl at his nod. "You'd better go deal with it and then come back so we can finish what we started."

CHAPTER 5

"*W*hat the fuck are you going to do about that skin?"

Dean sighed as Anderson started yelling demands before his ass had even cleared the frame. One day he was going to put a deadbolt on the door to make all assholes like Anderson book appointments to see him.

Reason for meeting: whine number seventy billion about how bears are superior and should rule the humans? Check. Round fucking file.

A pleasant fantasy about dragging Anderson out into the pit and beating the ever-loving crap out of him simmering in the back of his head, Dean gave the man a hard look.

As usual when dealing with his Prime, Anderson

was in full sheriff costume. It was almost as though he thought the symbols of human law enforcement would make one iota of difference in bear territory.

It didn't. Instead it made Dean want to laugh and ask where the fancy dress party was. That probably wouldn't help, so he didn't. But he didn't miss the fact that most of Anderson's little clique wore uniforms where ever they could, be that their leader's sheriff getup, various veterans' uniforms, probably down to boy scout uniforms if they didn't have anything better.

It would make him chuckle if it wasn't so pathetic. It was a blatantly transparent attempt to bolster their collective ego by making themselves look meaner and tougher than they really were.

Hell, if he and Morgan wore *their* uniforms... But that would never happen. Sure, they had them. Somewhere. He was fairly sure they had a rack of medals apiece as well, but damned if he remembered what they were. Their unit hadn't been the sort that wore fancy uniforms a lot, and bringing everyone in their unit home after each mission was worth more to them than a whole chest full of medals.

"Which of the humans put a bug up your ass now?" His answer was a growl as he ran his hand through his hair and suppressed a sigh. He hated that term for humans. It was insulting and racist, two things he'd been brought up not to be. "And you're the damn sheriff. Why come to me?"

"Not the humans." Anderson's lip curled back into a sneer. He might have been sheriff for the town, but no one in the clan was under any misconception he'd sought the position to protect and serve, or to uphold human laws.

The guy was a power junkie, pure and simple. When he couldn't get that power in the clan, refused a position as enforcer by Dean's father and then Dean himself when he'd become Prime, he'd gone out and gotten it another way.

"I'm talking about that damn skin, *Creed*." He spat the name, his voice dripping with hatred and contempt.

Dean arched an eyebrow, his expression neutral as he faced down the angry sheriff. "Exactly what do you want me to do about him? And for what reason? As far as I'm aware, he's broken no clan rules."

Anderson had been pacing Dean's office, but he now whirled on his heel to face Dean. His skin was flushed scarlet with anger, a very unfortunate color that clashed with his ginger hair, and a tiny vein pulsed in his temple.

"He *cheated!*" Spittle flew from the corner of his

lips, the expression in his eyes almost maniacal. "There's no way a half-skin like that could take on a full bear like Harrison and win. He cheated. There's no other explanation for it!"

"Really now?" Dean folded his arms over his broad chest, his feet shoulder-width apart as though he were back on the parade square. It was almost the at ease posture, but only an idiot would think Dean was relaxed. He was an alpha, an alpha of alphas. He could shift and have his jaws around Anderson's throat before the other man could blink. "Cheated? In the pit, in front of us all?"

"*Yes! Finally!*" Anderson threw his hands in the air. "You're seeing sense now. There's no *way* he could have won that bout."

Dean's voice was low and dangerous. "You mean the bout where Harrison attacked him from behind *after* he'd been beaten, using poison on his claws?"

Anderson wasn't stupid. At least not *stupid* stupid. At Dean's words he paused, his expression altering subtly. "That's got nothing to do with it. That was after. Creed shouldn't have won at all."

"And why is that, Elijah? Because you'd already decided that your man would win? But just to be on the safe side, you and Harrison decided to cook up a Plan B?"

The sheriff's mouth opened and closed, but no sound emerged. Dean didn't expect it to. If the guy was sensible, he'd realize that he was a hairsbreadth from incriminating himself. Conspiracy to alter the course of a pit challenge would land him in the thing himself, facing off against Dean. He might have an overinflated sense of his own importance, but he wasn't suicidal.

"I suggest you go away and think about your view of reality," Dean invited softly. "And come back when you're ready to play with the grown-ups."

The growl rumbled up from the center of Anderson's chest, his eyes suddenly dark. Tension shimmered through the air, fur poking over the top of the sheriff's collar and on the backs of his hands.

Dean took a step forward, his bear ready for some action. This asshole had pulled him out of Kacie's arms and he'd happily channel all that frustration into teaching the guy a lesson.

"Do it, Elijah," he invited softly. "Make my day."

The silence stretched out between them, the potential for violence thickening the air. Dean curled his lip back, letting a growl trickle between his teeth. If Anderson wanted to end this here and now, he was more than happy to.

But the sheriff flinched, looking away as he mumbled. "No offense meant, Prime."

Fucking little—

A knock on the door behind dragged Dean's attention away from the cowering bear in front of him, sudden fear rolling off him in waves.

"Yes, what is it?" he snapped, turning to find Bennett framed in the doorway. One look set all his alarm bells ringing. The normally laid back man looked agitated, worried even, a hand shoving his hair back as he looked at Dean.

"It's the Watson girls, boss. Someone got in, killed the babysitter, and took them."

"WHAT?"

Dean's roar of rage reverberated through the house, shaking the walls. Kacie stopped dead at the bottom of the stairs and lifted her head, using the sound to work out where he was. After it had become obvious he wasn't coming back, she'd dressed quickly and headed downstairs to find food.

But at the sound of him bellowing, her hunger fled and she barreled through the house, no thought in her mind but to get to him. Something was wrong, *very* wrong. She felt it in her bones.

What could be more wrong than being attacked by werebears in an alley? The little voice in the back of her head demanded. *Or finding out half the damn town get furry every month?*

She ignored it, beating feet through the room where she'd awakened on the dining table, and zeroed in on voices filtering through a partially open door she hadn't noticed before.

"What's wrong?" she asked, pushing it open to reveal Dean, Sheriff Anderson and Bennett Allan, a young guy from town who worked in the car shop not far from her house.

Surprise filled her. If they were here, in this room, it meant they were werebears and she'd never in a million years have picked the sheriff as one. He was the stereotype of the old boys' network, so set in his ways that you could set your watch by him. They *had* set their watches by him when they were children... knowing exactly where he'd be on his patrol route at any particular time of day. Made it easy for them to get up to the tricks kids did in a backwater town did without getting into trouble. But a bear? That blew her mind.

"Two kids have been kidnapped." Dean's words robbed her of breath for a second.

"Shit. For real? Who?"

"Yeah. Two of Jeb Watson's girls." Dean turned to the two men in the room. "Anderson, you'll need to run interference with the humans on this. We can't let them know it's bear business. Bennett, tell me everything you know."

Even as he rattled off orders with the air of someone accustomed to giving them, Dean had his cell in his hand, punching numbers. Holding a hand up to halt Bennett's report for a second, he held it up to his ear as Anderson scuttled out of the room.

"Braun, it's me. We got problems. Someone killed the Watsons' babysitter and lifted two of the kids... yeah, might be the rogues. Get teams out, search the town and outlying areas. I'm going to head down to the Watsons' and check it out."

Kacie sagged against the doorframe feeling like the bottom had just dropped out of her stomach. "Someone got killed?"

"Yeah. Angela Russell, the daughter of one of the Watsons' neighbors," Bennett answered her, his deep voice shaking as he paced the room. "She was a good kid, Prime, put up a fight. She didn't deserve what they did to her."

Kacie was swept along with Dean and Bennett as they headed out to the car. Her eyes widened as, on the way, they passed through the rest of the building. Either Dean lived in a damn mansion, or there were a lot more people who lived here.

She didn't get the chance to ask. Dean started one call as soon as he'd finished the last, his cell glued to his ear as he threw Bennett his keys. As the other man didn't lift an eyebrow, she assumed that driving his... his what? his boss'... car was nothing new.

Sliding into the back seat, she buckled up automatically—a fact she was glad about when Bennett hit the gas and the powerful vehicle sped off down the mountain road. He handled the big SUV like it was a race car, almost taking some corners on two wheels in complete disregard for both their personal safety and road law. All of them.

Not normally a nervous passenger, she was nonetheless reduced to clinging to the "oh shit" handle above the door and trying not to squeak as she was rattled around like a cookie in a jar. She closed her eyes tightly at one particularly hair-raising corner. A soon-to-be broken cookie if Bennett carried on driving like this.

Dean must have caught her small squeak of pain

as the vehicle slid to the side again, slamming her broadside into the door, and he turned on the driver.

"Slow down, Bennett. Human in the car, remember?"

Bennett grunted, casting her a glance in the rearview mirror. "Sorry, boss lady. I'll slow it down a bit."

She shook her head. "Don't mind me. Missing girls are way more important than my comfort. You just get us where we need to be."

Warmth and a look of approval crossed both men's faces at her words, the vehicle carrying on at a just slightly reduced breakneck speed. Kacie clung to the handle, trying to concentrate on the scenery around them, but thoughts of Angela filled her head.

"Was she... Angela Russell, I mean... was she killed by the same men who attacked me?" she asked suddenly.

Bennett nodded. "Think so. Smelled like it anyway."

Smelled like it? With those three little words Kacie was thrust back into a world that was so unlike the one she was used to. One that looked identical, yet was so different. A world where people could be identified by scent rather than sight, and men with claws attacked women in alleyways or in the safety of their own homes. Well, okay so Angela hadn't been in her own home, but she was babysitting so she might as well have been. And those girls had been taken from their home…

Rage built up inside her. It started with a small ball of heat at the center of her being but festered and grew the closer they got to town. The memory of claws flashing in the darkness made her stomach clench in remembered pain, and the anger exploded outward. It raced through her body in an instant, infecting each cell like wildfire until it consumed her. She clung harder to the handle above the door, her teeth clenched so tightly she was sure they were about to break off. Without warning, a feral growl rolled up from the center of her chest.

The two men in the front of the vehicle started in surprise, Dean turning to look at her.

"What?" she demanded. "You think you bears have the monopoly on viciousness? These guys took little girls… we find 'em, I want an hour alone in a room with them." She growled again, giving voice to her rage. "I'll teach 'em not to pick on women."

Dean nodded, a small smile on his face as the car pulled to a stop outside the Watson place. "You know what? I think that would be a lesson they wouldn't soon forget."

. . .

THERE WERE cars surrounding the Watson house when they arrived, vehicles from the sheriff's department as well as one she recognized. Lilly's little pink SUV was parked behind one of the police cars, the woman herself talking to a couple of men from town.

Relief rolling through her, Kacie slid from the back of Dean's car and headed over to her friend's side. Lilly turned from her conversation, and her eyes widened as she saw Kacie. The next instant, she was wrapped up in the tightest hug she'd ever been given.

"Ohmigod, Kace, I thought we'd lost you," Lilly whispered when the pair had finished squealing. "When those rogues attacked... there was so much blood."

Lilly released her grip a little and looked down at Kacie, which was when she realized exactly what was different about her friend. She held herself like Dean did.

"You're one of them, aren't you?"

Lilly's expression was worried, and she nibbled on her lower lip. "Yes, I am."

"Fuck's sake, Lilly!" Kacie broke away to run a

hand through her hair, turning in a circle before looking at the other woman again. "How am I the last to know about this?" She peered at Lilly intently. "*YOU*? A bear? You faint if you get so much as a paper cut!"

Lilly shrugged, looking sheepish. "I really hate paper cuts? The way the paper slices through your skin..." She shuddered. "It's horrible."

Kacie shook her head. Lilly was actually going pale at the very thought of a little paper cut. Amazing.

"But... a bear?" She blinked as some of the memories from that night melded together and made more sense. "You fought them off, didn't you? You saved me. You and Kait. Oh hell, is Kait a bear too? Is that why she disappeared off to the city? Some secret bear business?"

"No, not at all. Kait's as human as you are." Lilly chuckled, shaking her head. "She did help, though, when we were attacked."

It felt like the blood drained completely from Kacie's body. "Oh hell, is she okay? If she's not a bear... Did those assholes hurt her?"

"She's perfectly fine, I promise." Lilly smiled, reaching out to give her upper arm a reassuring squeeze.

"They're still out there though… we have to fetch her, make sure she's okay."

"Oh, she's fine, believe me," Lilly chuckled. "She's with Creed, and now he's finally gotten her, there's no way he'll let anyone hurt her. Ever."

Kacie's eyes widened at the hint of gossip. "Kait and Creed? No way!"

"I know! It's great, isn't it?" Lilly's grin of happiness for their friend said everything. Then movement behind Kacie caught her attention and her expression became serious. "We'll catch up later, hon. I've got work to do."

"Go." Kacie shooed her away. "Go do whatever it is you bears need to do. But… girly night in and you give me all the gossip. Soon."

Lilly threw a grin over her shoulder. "Deal."

CHAPTER 6

The instant Dean strode into the Watsons' home after speaking to the bears outside, he was assaulted by the scent of blood and unfamiliar bears. He paused for a second, curling his lip back from his teeth as he breathed in to study them.

Five males, all unfamiliar... He growled, the rumble of pure rage made into sound. These males had invaded his territory, killed a human under his protection and taken two bear females from his clan. And if that wasn't enough to seal their fate, they'd also hurt his fated mate.

He bunched his fists, his claws aching to burst free. They might be walking and talking, breathing and all that, but they were dead. They just didn't know it yet.

"Prime?" The girl's mother, Elisa Watson, stood in front of him, her youngest child held tightly. Her expression was haunted, eyes red-rimmed from tears. "Thank the moon. Please... you have to get my babies back. They... Angela..."

He took her by the upper arms, expression open and determined. "We will get them back, Elisa. You have my word as Prime on that."

"Thank you," the woman whispered, tears welling in her eyes again. She didn't ask anything else, didn't need to. He was Prime and he'd given his word. Her children would be found, or he would die trying.

And that was where assholes like Anderson went wrong. They pursued power for its own sake. They wanted people at their beck and call, looking up to them, and to issue orders. They forgot that a Prime was not a free bear. Forgot that the Prime didn't only lead the clan, he *served* the clan as well. His word was law, but it was also his bond. And no Prime could ever break that.

"Mrs. Watson? Hi, I'm Kacie. How about I make you a nice hot drink and we'll let the..." she paused for a moment, flicking a glance around the room.

Anderson and his deputies were already in the next room, where the scent of blood was the strongest, but other bears were already here, waiting Dean's orders. She didn't skip a beat though. "And we'll let the Prime and his associates deal with the sheriff, shall we?"

A hand under the terrified mother's arm, Kacie led her away into the kitchen, throwing a small smile over her shoulder at Dean.

"You got a keeper there," Bennett said quietly. "Never seen any newbie accept the bear-life quite so easily."

Dean's chest puffed out a little with pride. "Well, she's a Beauty girl, born and bred, plus she's my fated. What else did you expect?"

The two men walked through the main room, where what remained of Dean's humor fled. Framed by the comfortable civility of the Watsons' home, with its hardwearing cord and leather couches, and cozy throws, was a scene right out of a horror movie.

In silence, he studied the room, noting every splash of blood, every handprint, every claw mark and bite in soft, undefended flesh. Like all bears, Dean had been born a shifter, but he'd always been aware of real bears. There were a few in the Beauty territory. Mostly, they avoided wereclan areas, but occasionally they stayed. So he knew what a natural bear kill looked like.

Kill was the operative word. Bears were animals. They killed to eat or to defend themselves. There was no malice in what they did.

This wasn't a natural bear kill. The human girl, Angela Russell, hadn't been killed. She'd been slaughtered in cold blood. She lay on her back on the coffee table like an offering, her face serene. That's where the peaceful image ended. Below the neck, her clothes and her skin were shredded and covered in blood. The stark white of broken ribs was the only relief in the wash of scarlet.

Disgust and rage rose hard and fast. She hadn't just been killed, she'd been tortured first. *Played* with.

He snarled, a low, rumbling sound that promised vengeance and hell when he caught up with who was responsible.

This shit did not happen. Not on his watch.

"Oh...Holy shit." Morgan cursed as he walked in, obviously unprepared for the sight of the murdered girl spread out like an offering. "Fuck's sake, you could've warned me. Human sense of smell, remember?"

"Sorry, bud," Dean rumbled quietly. "Still taking it in myself."

"Understandable." Just like that Morgan locked down, his expression turning purely professional as he studied the scene. "More than one bear. And it looks like she put up a good fight. I might be able to pick up something from blood traces, but it's going to take me a while to filter through her blood. Spells are good, but they aren't that good."

Dean shook his head. "We don't have the time for that. They've taken two girls and we need them back, yesterday. You got anything else?"

"Girls? How old?"

"Four and seven," a hoarse voice answered from the doorway. Jeb Watson stood framed there, the big man's face haunted. Dean noted how he avoided looking at the scene beyond the two men, and he moved subtly so the man wouldn't see. Angela wasn't his daughter, but these bastards had his two children. Dean knew without a shadow of a doubt that if Jeb saw the body, all he'd see was his daughters lying there instead. Just as all he could see was Kacie…

"Good." Morgan nodded. "Then chances are they still sleep with teddy bears? Yes?"

Jeb nodded dully, forcing his attention from Dean to the big warlock. "Yeah, they do. Why?"

"Bring them to me. I might just have a way to track your daughters down before any harm comes to them."

MRS. WATSON WAS IN SHOCK, but she was still mistress of her own kitchen. She wouldn't let Kacie do anything, firmly sitting her down in the corner while she bustled around, making coffee for the men in the house. Her expression was strained but she kept up a light stream of chatter, mostly about town business rather than what was going on in the next room, or, interestingly, anything to do with bears.

Thankfully, no one would let her leave the kitchen to deliver drinks. Instead, as soon as a load of drinks were ready, there somehow seemed to be someone in the doorway waiting. Kacie had no doubt they knew, that somehow they could hear the kettle coming to the boil each time. Except the last time, when Mrs. Watson…Elisa…had gotten a feed ready for the baby, Poppy. As she settled down to feed her, the baby held snugly and firmly in her arms, the door opened again.

Kacie breathed a sigh of relief to see Dean waiting there. Excusing herself from the kitchen for a moment, she slid through the door into the corridor to join him.

"Hey," she said softly, studying his expression. He looked weary, like bone-deep tired, and worried. "How's it going out there?"

He didn't answer straight away, moving them both closer to the wall as the sheriff's men wheeled a gurney out of the front room, a zipped up black body bag strapped to it. Sadness welled deep in her chest. Angela had been so young. A student home for the holidays, Kacie remembered her being a vivacious girl with her whole life ahead of her.

Dean sighed. "As well as can be expected."

Need tightened his features and he reached out to pull her into his arms. She didn't argue. Simply stepped into his embrace and let him wrap her up. Nestled against his hard, strong body like this, she felt safe. Protected. Tears prickled in the backs of her eyes. It could so easily have been her in the body bag and she felt awful that she was glad it wasn't. Not that Angela deserved to be, but if it had been, she'd never have found out that Dean felt the same way about her as she did about him. Had for years.

Pulling back, he looked down into her face. He

didn't speak. Instead, he reached up and brushed his thumb over her lower lip. She murmured in pleasure as his lips covered hers. The kiss was soft and gentle, more about giving and receiving comfort than raw passion, but she didn't care. She clung to him, eager for anything he had to give. For any touch he gifted her with.

This, them, was the one thing she could hold onto in this whole situation that she actually understood. She'd always had a thing for him, as long back as she could remember. Had always felt they had some kind of connection, even if he didn't seem to notice her.

His response earlier and the way he held her now, as though she was precious and delicate...no *way* had he not noticed her. He had to have been ignoring her. That stung, more than she cared to admit, but she was quick to excuse his behavior in her mind. Perhaps there were rules about humans and bears.

The thoughts were swept away, though, as the kiss deepened, and she was lost to sensual bliss. She'd been kissed before, but never like this. Never with the same intensity of passion Dean managed to pack into each and every little touch. As though he had to hold himself back whenever he was around her.

It was exhilarating, addictive and kind of a little scary all at the same time. Especially now that she knew what lay hidden inside him. She caught her breath as he broke the kiss, a little sound of disappointment in the back of her throat.

He leaned his forehead against hers, his eyes closed but his voice low and full of regret.

"We can't do this here."

"Why not?" she whispered back, smoothing her hands over his broad shoulders. She would never get tired of touching him. She just wanted to touch him with much less on, and preferably somewhere more private. "We're only kissing. Not even making out properly."

He lifted his head, eyes dark with a heat that made her shiver. "Sweetheart, we won't stay *just* kissing for long. I promise you."

"Oh...*ohhh.*"

He smiled at her little gasp and dropped a kiss on her forehead. "We'll pick this up later. I just came to tell you I have to go. We found a way to track the girls."

Relief flooded her. "Awesome. What are we waiting for?"

Dean shook his head. "Not we. Me. You can't come, sweetheart. It's too dangerous."

"What the fuck? You're kidding me?" She gave him a sharp look, hardly believing what she was hearing. "These assholes attacked Lilly, Kait and me in the alley, right?"

"Yes. We believe so."

"Then screw that." Determination filled her, and she stood up to her full height. Which, if she was honest, was itty bitty compared to Dean's well-over six-foot frame. She could kick them in the ankles. She didn't care. "Get me a baseball bat or something because I want some payback. I'll teach them not to pick on women or little girls... assholes!"

"My little mate. So brave and fierce." He shook his head, bending to steal another kiss that stole her breath. His expression dropped serious when he pulled away. "But I can't let you go, Kacie. You're my fated."

"Bullshit," she tried to snap back, but her voice emerged way too soft and breathy. "Fated, what does that even mean anyway?"

He slid his hand into her hair, palm cradling the side of her neck gently. The look on his face was so achingly tender and fiercely protective it brought tears to her eyes, stopping her planned argument right in its tracks.

"It means that you're it for me, sweetheart. Without you, that's it, I can't go on... You're my reason to live."

Holy shit. She blinked and nodded, speechless.

And to think she'd just been hoping for an "I like you."

She could really get used to this bear thing...

"Turn left just up here."

Dean hit the brakes at the command, swinging the SUV into the turn and hitting the gas again. "Where now? Carry on?"

The tension in the car was high, what with three shifters and Morgan crammed into a space not really suited for such big men, humans or otherwise. Magic warred with shift potential, turning the air almost too thick to breathe. Gunning the vehicle down the road ahead, he cast a glance over his shoulder.

Watson and Morgan sat in the back, a map spread over their laps. The big warlock clutched a teddy bear, his free hand held tightly clenched over the map as it steadily dripped blood. Jeb leaned in, relaying where the drops fell. "Right. Right here. Now!" he barked.

"Fuck it," Dean growled as they passed the turn. "Bit more warning would help, guys!"

Slamming the brakes on, he swung around in a squeal of tires and swerved to avoid the cars following. Now they had a lead on where the Watson girls were, the clan was out in force to get them back.

"Doing the best I can," Morgan replied, his voice tight with strain. "It's not like fucking GPS, you know."

"I know, bud." Instantly Dean apologized. They were lucky to have Morgan around, and he knew that. It gave them an edge other clans just didn't have. "You're doing great."

Morgan snorted in amusement. "I know. I'm the fucking bomb, and don't you forget it."

"Not likely, you never freaking let up about it."

"Keep going," Jeb ordered as they passed a few more roads. Dean frowned as they left town. He'd been sure they'd be headed to one of the outlying properties, but this road didn't lead anywhere but up to...

"It's the old Black property," Bennett breathed as

realization hit him as well. "It's the only thing up here for miles."

"Yeah, it's gotta be." Putting his foot down, Dean gunned the engine, hoping they weren't too late.

It took them less than five minutes to reach the small farmhouse they were headed for. Abandoned for years, it had belonged to one of the clan's older bears, but he'd passed on a few years ago. As far as Dean knew, no one had lived there since. It certainly looked abandoned as they hurtled up the driveway to screech to a halt outside the small group of buildings. There was a house, a few feed sheds and a small barn. Boards nailed over the smashed windows and rubbish piled up against the walls of the house told a tale of neglect. Not surprising. Properties out here in the back end of beyond weren't exactly sought after. But, not his problem. Getting Jeb's girls back was and they could be in any one of the buildings.

"Main house," he ordered, catching the hint of movement behind a boarded window as he shoved his door open.

At his movement, the amassed clan poured out of the cars behind Dean's, some before the wheels had even stopped. Feet and massive paws hit the hard-packed dirt as roars filled the air. They were met by answering snarls and roars from within the buildings as the rogues answered. The first of them appeared in the doorway of the house. Fully shifted, his massive form filled the frame as he snarled at the newcomers.

Dean grinned, feeling the familiar surge of adrenaline as he let go of his human form. His bear ripped free, and less than a second later he charged down the bear in the doorway, leaving the man left in him to chuckle mentally at the rogue's look of stunned surprise. He was alpha, he was Prime... there wasn't a bear in the clan that could shift quicker than he could. He barreled into the other bear, using his momentum as an extra weapon. He might have been a little smaller in frame than his opponent, but he was a mean-ass son of a bitch when it came to a fight—furry or not. He moved faster than a bear of his size should be able to, slashing fur with his claws and trying to get a hold.

The rogue defended, moving to back up into the corridor behind the door but Dean wasn't having any of that. Rising on his back feet, he left his belly undefended for a second to slam his weight down on the rogue's muzzle. The unexpected slap-down took the other bear by surprise and he stumbled. Dean was on him in a heartbeat, his teeth buried in the thick muscle and fur at the back of his opponent's neck. In a move not unlike a mother-cat with her kittens, he dragged the rogue out of the doorway and flung him in the dirt in front of the house.

The bear rolled, on his feet in an instant to roar defiance at Dean, but the Prime just growled in amusement. The male could roar and bluster all he liked. He was going nowhere. The door now cleared, two clan bears surged through the gap to get the girls. Lilly and Jeb, both fully shifted, were more than capable of dealing with any bears still in the house. He actually felt sorry for them. Braun was mean as fuck when she was mad, and there was nothing that got her more pissed off than people hurting kids. And Jeb... he didn't actually want to think what Jeb would do to them. One thing was for certain, it was no less than they deserved for taking the man's kids.

He circled the big bear, ignoring all the other fights that were going on around them. There weren't that many, certainly not as many as he'd thought there would be for a pack like this. Rogues weren't usually a problem. Normally male, they tended to flit from pack to pack until they found one that would take them in. But if they banded together like this, *then* they became a problem, if not a right royal pain in the ass. The rest must be inside with the girls, he decided, and launched his attack.

This time he didn't mess about. He didn't have to worry about the male creating a bottleneck, or worse, crushing a child. Instead, he had all the space in the world and a roaring need to taste this guy's blood in the back of his throat. One moment he was pacing, circling, and the next he launched himself forward. His huge paws hit the dirt twice, a gallop before he threw himself on the male's back, grappling around his ribs with razor-sharp claws.

The rogue started in surprise. He roared as he bucked and shook himself, trying to throw Dean off. But Dean had a good grip, biting down on his opponent's neck as he threw himself to the side. The bear staggered but stayed upright. Bear tipping, Morgan had called the move once when he'd seen Dean fight, and the name had stuck. Curling his lips back, he roared around his teeth buried in the male's neck and heaved himself to the other side. This time it worked. The rogue lost his footing and slid. Dean moved like lightning, man and bear in total accord. In less than half a second, he had his jaws locked around the rogue's throat and bit down.

The rogue managed an aborted whine, but then blood gushed and flesh parted. Dean shook his head, feeling the blood flow over his snout. Fucking rogues, they'd learn not to mess with clan territory.

"We got them," Braun's voice rang out from the house.

Dropping his opponent to bleed his last in the dust, Dean stepped back. Braun stood in the doorway, ushering Jeb out of the house. The big man held a girl in each arm, tears flowing down his face. Dean breathed a sigh of relief. They were safe, and unharmed by the look of it. Between one step and the next he went from bear to man, looking at Lilly as she walked toward him. The fact that they were both as naked as the day they were born didn't register with either of them. Bears soon lost any modesty about their bodies when they learned to shift.

"How many of them were there?" he asked, noticing Braun's frown.

"That's just it. There weren't any in there, just the girls. It seems way too easy..." Her eyes widened as Dean growled.

"It's a fucking distraction."

CHAPTER 7

*K*acie had known Mrs. Watson most of her life. Not in a best buds type of way, but she'd seen her around town or picking her girls up from the nursery, chatted with her in the supermarket, that type of thing. She seemed… normal. The wholesome soccer mom type. Nothing out of the ordinary. Never once had she given any indication that she wasn't even human.

"So, how are you holding up with all this?" Elisa asked as she bustled around the kitchen making coffee. It was the third cup she'd made them, the two previous having gone cold while she found something else to clean or tidy.

"This?" Arms full of giggling baby, Kacie paused for a moment with a frown, unsure what Mrs.

Watson meant. She wasn't the one who'd had a girl killed in her own home or her children kidnapped, yet Elisa was asking how *she* was?

"Finding out about bears, dear. It must be strange to suddenly have all that dumped on you."

"Oh, yes. A little." She breathed a sigh of relief. So far Elisa seemed to be holding up well under the strain, and she was more than happy to focus on her own circumstances if it took the woman's mind off her own predicament.

"Being honest, I thought it was all a dream at first. I mean, come on. Werebears?" She smiled and shrugged. "No offense but it's like something out of a book or a film, isn't it?"

"Yeah, it is a bit. It's just something I grew up with so I've never known anything else. Our males don't tend to look as good as the werewolves on screen, but I sure wouldn't mind some eye candy like that around. No siree." Elisa chuckled as she moved the tea and coffee canisters, cleaning behind them for the umpteenth time. Kacie recognized the habitual motion, the need to do something, whatever it was, to keep her mind off what was going on.

The baby giggled, big dark eyes fixed on Kacie for a moment before she made a grab for a wayward curl. "Hey, hey… whatcha doin'?" she smiled, pretending to try and tug the strand of hair back. The baby just giggled and held tighter.

"She likes you," Elisa commented, watching from the other side of the kitchen. "You're good with kids."

Kacie smiled, her attention caught for a moment as something moved outside, just visible over Elisa's shoulder, but when she focused, nothing was there. Must have been a branch moving in the wind, she decided, and focused on the other woman. "Thank you. Always wanted some of my own. Maybe one day."

Elisa chuckled as she lifted her mug to her lips and blew the steam off the surface. "Oh, Dean'll want kids. Probably sooner rather than later too."

Oh hell, that was a little personal. Were bears always this blunt? Hiding her surprise, Kacie tried a smile despite her discomfort. "It's a bit early for that. We only just got together—" If one hot encounter in Dean's bedroom could be considered "getting together." She hoped so though. God, she was pathetic because she *really* hoped so. "—I don't know if we'll even last yet."

Elisa froze, mug halfway to her lips and looked

over the rim. It was a wary look, one that set an alarm off in the back of Kacie's mind.

"You don't know, do you?" Elisa asked softly.

Kacie frowned, recovering her hair from the baby's grip. "Know what? About Dean being this Prime thing? It means he's your boss... the boss of all the bears in the town?"

She hadn't been told as much, but she wasn't daft. It had been easy to work out that Dean wasn't your average run of the mill bear. He was something special.

"Not that, no." The other woman shook her head, putting her mug down on the side. For a second there was movement in the gathering darkness outside, but Kacie ignored it. She had far more to worry about than some branch swaying in the breeze.

"Although, yes, you got it right. The Prime is what we call the leader of a bear clan. Dean's our Prime, as was his father before him. It doesn't always run in families though. Anyone can challenge a Prime for his position. If he wins... new leadership," she explained. "But that wasn't what I meant. Did Dean explain what happens when a human finds out about us?"

"They freak out and end up in the mental unit?"

Kacie ventured. "Because I was sure that's where I was headed."

Elisa didn't chuckle. Her expression was worried and her face pale. "No, it's worse than that. The only type of human that knows about us is one who is mated to a bear. If not…"

Unease rolled up Kacie's spine like a snake slithering through long grass. "If not?"

Elisa met her gaze. "Then they have to die."

Kacie opened her mouth, but no sound came out. This was serious shit. Clearing her throat, she went to speak again, sure Elisa had it wrong, but she didn't get chance.

Instead, the kitchen window exploded inward, covering them in shattered glass. A huge bear landed on the counter, its claws digging into the surface and cracking the sink.

Elisa turned, shoving Kacie and the baby in her arms toward the doorway in one movement. Her eyes were dark with determination and something else as fur began to spread over her face.

"*Run.*"

KACIE DIDN'T ARGUE. Instead, she tucked the baby

close, and for the first time in her life, she did exactly as she was told.

She ran.

Racing down the corridor toward the front door, she had a hand out to turn the latch and throw it open when the window to the side shattered. She screamed, half turning and throwing her arm up to protect both her head and baby Poppy. A large, furred paw tipped with razor-sharp claws shoved through the gap, fishing through the air as though looking for them.

The bear it belonged to snarled, peering through the gap between its leg and the wooden frame. All too human intelligence shone in the near-black eyes. She swallowed hard, reading her own death there. Snarls and crashes rang from the kitchen but Kacie wasn't stupid enough to think that Elisa could hold the big bear off for long.

The sound of breaking glass in the living room made Kacie shrink back against the wall. They were everywhere. There was no way to escape. Tears of frustration welled up, panic trying to consume her.

"No." The word was clear, firm and quite unexpected. She looked down at the baby in her arms, Poppy looking back calmly. "This is not happening. We are getting out of this, you hear me?"

Determination filling her, she turned on her heel and raced up the stairs. More windows broke near the back of the house and lent wings to her heels. She didn't know much about bears, but stairs had to slow any animal down, surely?

Reaching the short landing, she grabbed at anything she could as she went. The bookcase at the top of the stairs, a drying rack full of laundry, the tallboy near one of the girls' bedrooms, they all went tumbling over as adrenaline lent Kacie the kind of strength that allowed mothers to lift small cars off their children.

Reaching the master bedroom, she slammed the door behind them and dropped Poppy onto the bed. The baby bounced, giggling, but Kacie had already spun on her heel to start dragging the heavy chest of drawers across the door. Her heart pounded as she heaved but she managed it and stepped back. The piece was antique and weighed what felt like a ton, but she suspected it wouldn't give them much time.

Crap, she needed something else.

Racing to the window, she looked out. Instantly, she shrank back. Hard-faced men thronged around the building, and they didn't look like they were hoping to borrow a cup of sugar.

"Fuck." She shoved a hand through her hair,

raking it back from her face. "You got this, Kacie. Think."

Something big crashed against the door to the bedroom, moving the heavy chest a fraction. Swallowing her squeak, she grabbed the baby off the bed. She needed to do something, like in the next thirty seconds, or they were both dead. Casting a frantic glance around the room, she dropped to her knees and shoved the baby under the bed. The gap was small, almost too small, and she smiled at Poppy.

"It's going to be okay, sweetie. You'll be fine, just keep quiet. Shhhh, okay?" Giving the baby a last stroke on the cheek, Kacie stood up and smoothed the bedding back down so it hung straight. The bed was big and heavy, even a bear would have trouble moving it. Poppy would be safe.

Her? Not so much. Her lip wavered, but she caught it between her teeth, determined to face this with the strength and fierceness Dean had seen in her.

Dean. At the thought of the big, former soldier werebear... Prime, whatever he was, tears welled up and spilled over her eyelashes. At least she'd gotten to kiss him, even if a life together, hell even a hot couple of years together, was out of the question. He was hers, and she his. Always had been, and always would be, to her last breath.

The door slammed again. She jumped, a small cry on her lips when the chest slid half an inch. A weapon, she needed a weapon. Looking around she came up with nothing until her gaze swept to the wall over the bed.

Bingo.

Two samurai swords hung there in their sheaths.

"Jeb Watson," she whispered. "I think I love you."

Clambering on the bed, she grabbed the handles and yanked one of the swords free. It came away easily and she slid it free of the sheath. It was dull. A fake sword. The bottom dropped out of her stomach as the bear hit the other side of the door again. She was about to face down hundreds of pounds of apex predator with what amounted to little more than a metal stick. And to think, Dean had made her stay behind because it was safer.

"Fuck my life."

DEAN HAD NEVER DRIVEN SO FAST in all his life, not even when he was on active service with the enemy shooting at him. He rammed the pedal down as far as it would go, the big engine roaring as the SUV sped down the road at breakneck speed. It was well above the limit but he didn't care. Anderson would just have to arrest him. Or try to anyway. A growl trickled from his throat. If the guy tried to get between him and his fated, he'd be facing Dean in the pit. And he wouldn't be walking away.

The car was full, Morgan in the front seat and three bears—Lilly, Bennett and another of the younger enforcers—crammed into the back seat. They were all silent. Grim-faced. The fight at the Black place had been too easy. Dean swore, slamming his hand into the wheel.

"Should've known it was a distraction."

"Don't beat yourself up about it. We were all suckered in," Morgan murmured, clinging to the 'oh shit' handle as Dean swung the SUV into the road the Watsons lived on. The house was right at the end of the street, backing onto countryside, which was no surprise. Most bears picked property for its proximity to nature. It made the need to shift easier if all you needed to do to hit the woods was head down to the bottom of the garden.

Thankfully, Beauty was a sleepy town so there was no traffic on the road. They turned the last corner and the house came into view.

"Shit..." Lilly's shocked whisper said it all. The house was surrounded by bears; some were in human form, but some shifted as they climbed through shattered windows. One huge bear had just broken down the front door, its massive furred rump disappearing through the ruined wood.

The roar welled up directly from the center of Dean's soul, shaking his entire body with rage as he slid the SUV to a stop in a spray of stones and dust. He barely managed to put it in park, throwing the door open and leaping out.

The roar emerged then, a bellow of fury and challenge that every bear for miles around would hear. He didn't care. These assholes had broken the laws, showed themselves where humans could see them, and worse, they'd attacked his fated mate.

If she was dead... every fiber of his being shook with fury and fear... Then no bear would be safe. He would track down every single one of them and make them pay. Slowly. With agony and blood.

Storming toward the house, he let fur flow over his skin. A bear rounded the corner of the house and charged him. Body surging with power, Dean batted him aside with barely a thought, sending him flying to crash into the side of the house and slide down the clapboard with a soft groan.

He kicked the remains of the door aside and stepped through into the corridor. The place was trashed, glass and broken furniture everywhere. Behind him, he heard Lilly and her enforcers roar as they engaged the rogue bears.

Elisa Watson appeared in the kitchen doorway. Her hair was mussed, she was covered in blood and holding her arm close to her chest, but she was alive. From the look in her eyes, whichever bear had been unlucky enough to get caught in the kitchen with her hadn't been as fortunate.

"Upstairs," she said, starting toward him. "Kacie has Poppy. They're upstairs."

Dean didn't argue, catching Kacie's familiar scent in the corridor. Another, muskier scent covered his little mate's and his lips curled back from his teeth. Male. Bear. Near his mate... Still growling, he raced up the stairs, Elisa hot on his heels. They rounded the top of the stairs together, but Dean took point.

The corridor was short and narrow. At the end there was a bear blocking the door to one of the bedrooms. The door was smashed and broken, and from the look of it, he was trying to clamber over a chest of drawers that had been used to hold it shut. Every time he tried, though, there was a female yell and he roared, slipping back. As he did, Dean caught a glimpse of Kacie, something metallic in her hand. Relief hit him hard and fast. He'd feared the worst, imaging her broken body split open like the Russell girl's had been. All the way back he'd tortured himself, terrified he'd never see her smile again. Never hear her laugh. Never get to tell her that he loved her.

The realization blazed through him like a wildfire.

He loved her. He loved Kacie Leroy. Not just because she was his fated mate and belonged to him, but because of who she was. He loved her for her, not for what she was to him.

The door to their left opened, another of the rogues emerging. A growl behind him told him that Elisa was on the case and within a heartbeat, the woman had changed and charged down the rogue bear, lashing out viciously.

Hell hath no fury like a mamma bear, he thought, hearing the squeals of pain from Elisa's victim. *And ain't that the frigging truth.*

Dean carried on, all emotion leeching from him as he focused on the bear in front of him. It was the biggest he'd ever seen, even bigger than the one he'd taken down at the Black place, but that didn't matter. He broke into a run, using the powerful muscles in his thighs to propel him forward and then up into the air as he let the change rip through him.

This asshole had threatened his mate, which meant it was a dead bear walking. And right now, Dean was not just a Prime... he was the mother-fucking grim reaper.

And he was about to send a soul to hell.

CHAPTER 8

"*W*ill you just fuck off already?" Kacie hissed, as the bear at the door snarled at her.

Werebears were tenacious, she'd give them that. So far it had ripped through the top part of the door like it was little more than matchwood, rather than the solid wood she could see it was. But, somehow, some of the broken wood seemed to have slipped down between the ruins of the door and the chest, jamming it solidly and stopping the door from opening further.

Someone, somewhere loved her. Perhaps she'd been nice to fluffy kittens or someone in a previous life. She didn't know. Didn't care. She'd pray to any deity in the vicinity if they just kept that door jammed with the bear on the other side of it.

The bear snarled and shoved again. But the harder it pushed, the tighter the door jammed. So it tried a different tack. Hauling itself up, it tried to scramble over the top of the chest. It didn't work, the gap too small, but it wasn't giving up.

Each time it fell back, it snarled and pushed forward again. Its claws gouged deep gashes into the top of the chest as it scrabbled for purchase. The sight of the large bear trying to fit itself through the small gap made Kacie chuckle. It reminded her of her last shopping trip to the city, when her favorite clothing line had "re-evaluated" their sizing policy and everything ended up at least two sizes smaller. And with the generous booty she had? She'd needed lube and a shoe-horn to get into her regular size.

At least, the sight of a size four bear trying to squeeze into a size two gap *should* have been amusing. Should. If said bear wasn't taking swipes at her with razor sharp claws every chance it got. It roared at her and she grimaced at its breath.

"Seriously, dude, ever considered a breath mint?" She took a step back when a claw almost kissed the front of her shirt. "And would a bit of flossing be too much to ask? Dental hygiene is very important, you know."

It grunted, getting a hold on the chest with its claws and managing to inch forward through the gap. Triumph filled its black-on-black eyes.

Oh no, we're not having that. Dancing forward, she lashed out with the fake sword and smacked it soundly across the nose. It howled in pain and recoiled, sliding back through the gap to land on its ass with a thump.

"Ha! How'd you like them apples, furface?" she taunted through the gap as she waved the swords in threat. "And there's more where that came from."

Enraged, the bear tried again, backing up along the corridor to hurl itself at the gap, as though momentum would manage what brute strength hadn't. Kacie held her breath, sending up a quick prayer that it wouldn't.

Each time the bear surged forward, she smacked it again. Hard blows right on its nose. It kept coming, its expression becoming more and more enraged, and she knew it was only a matter of time. Sooner or later, her luck was going to run out. Either the chest was going to give from the bear's claws chewing it up, or some other bear was going to come crashing through the window behind her.

She cast a glance over her shoulder... shit, how well could bears climb?

A thin wail from under the bed made her head snap around, and she cooed soothingly in response. "Shhh, darling. It's going to be okay. You just go to sleep. It'll be fine."

Yeah, right, because god knows how many hundreds of pounds of bear wasn't trying to bust through the door to eat their faces off. Other than that, they were fine.

She smacked the bear again, barely managing to avoid its claws this time, but before it could gather itself for a new attack there was a roar behind it. Another bear appeared, leaping onto the back of the first and laying into it with claws and teeth.

She gasped, scrambling backward at the sheer viciousness of the attack. She hadn't seen a bear attack before, but she'd heard horror stories of hikers getting mauled. Like everyone in the local area, she'd read all the advice of protecting the softer parts of the body, like the stomach, while playing dead until the bear lost interest.

Obviously the first bear hadn't because he sure as hell wasn't playing dead. Instead, the two rolled over and around each other like some freakishly big ball of fur. Every so often a clawed paw would appear and slam into the other, or a snarling snout would rise above the fur, mouth open wide to take a bite. Within seconds, the white of both claws and teeth were stained red with blood.

Kacie held her breath, edging forward to watch the fight through the ruins of the door. It ranged down the corridor and back but it was obvious the first bear was seriously outmatched. The smaller one backed it up in the corner near the bathroom, claws flashing as they stabbed time after time into the other bear's ribcage.

It reared on its back legs, roaring in pain and fury as it tried to use its bulk to bring down its opponent. It didn't work. The smaller bear launched itself forward and up, teeth latching around the bigger bear's throat as it used its back claws to rip deeply, scrabbling at the unprotected stomach like a cat would disembowel its pray.

The big bear slumped, the light going out of its eyes as it slid down the wall to land in a furry heap. Kacie breathed a sigh of relief, staggering backward to sit heavily on the bed.

"Hey, help me with this."

Her head snapped up at Elisa's voice to find the other woman in the doorway, trying to shift the heavy chest. She was covered in blood with a vicious claw mark across her cheek. She looked like she'd been in a down and dirty fight.

"Holy shit. Are you okay?"

Elisa just grinned, something not human sparkling in the back of her eyes. "Yeah. I'm good. You should see the other guy."

Kacie had no choice but to smile back. She'd had no idea the quiet mother could be so vicious. But then, she'd had no idea that half the town were bears either.

"Was that... you out there?" she asked. "Remind me not to piss you off, okay?"

"Me? No, that was Dean," Elisa chuckled as the two women moved into place around the chest. It was a solid bit of furniture but its days of holding clothes were well and truly over. The top was a shredded mess of claw marks and broken wood, the frame twisted and half the drawers warped and broken, spilling their contents onto the floor.

Between them they managed to heave it out of the way, Elisa providing most of the grunt. As soon as it was clear of the door, she surged through the gap and into the room. Pausing just inside the door, she lifted her head and sniffed the air. It was such an animalistic movement that it took Kacie aback for a moment as she realized just how good the werebears were at concealing themselves. Now they didn't have to around her, she could see the differences in behavior.

Before Kacie could open her mouth to tell Elisa where her daughter was, the bear woman rounded the bed and dropped to her knees.

"Hey, Poppet," she murmured, lifting the valance to look underneath. "What'cha doing under there? Are you playing hide and seek without Mommy? No fair, you know how much Mommy *loves* hide and seek!"

Kacie watched, feeling like an interloper as Elisa cradled her baby daughter in her arms protectively. Her heart ached at the sight, and a deep longing welled up from within her.

She wanted that. Not Elisa's baby...but one of her own. She wanted to be a mother.

She wanted to be mother to Dean's children. Bears or not, she didn't care.

A soft shuffle on the carpet behind her made her turn, and she froze as a bear padded softly into the room. It was the one who had attacked the bear who had been trying to kill her. That was the only reason she didn't run when all her survival instincts were screaming at her to flee, to get as far away from the predator in front of her as she could.

She didn't move though. Instead, she forced herself to remain still as the bear approached. It stopped barely a handbreadth in front of her.

It. Was. Huge.

Not as big as the monster who'd tried to kill her, but that had to have been some sort of freakish mutant. This was certainly the biggest she'd ever been this close to. She stopped for a moment to think when she'd *ever* been this close to a bear. Maybe the humungous teddy at the air-rifle stands when the circus came to town... but that was it.

His fur was dark, almost black speckled with a dark brown, and he had a thick ruff of fur around his neck. His nose was black, with a deep gash across it that made her wince. His mouth was closed, concealing the sharp teeth she knew were within, and his expression was relaxed and nonthreatening. It didn't matter. Somewhere along the way her fear had disappeared.

Her gaze reached the bear's eyes and she gasped. Right there, in the dark orbs, she saw him. Saw Dean. It didn't matter that his eyes were bear dark rather than the hazel she was familiar with. She knew. She recognized him.

It was Dean.

It was the man she loved.

"You know, you didn't need to go and get a scar to try and impress me—"

Her voice broke and she collapsed to her knees, wrapping her arms tightly around his furry neck. "Oh god, Dean, I was so scared," she whispered, burying her face in his fur. It was both as coarse as she'd expected but somehow softer all at the same time. How that worked, she didn't know. Didn't care. All she knew was that it felt right.

She held on, even when the fur receded and the big shoulders changed shape.

"Shhh, I'm here now," he whispered, holding her close. "I'll never let anyone hurt you. Never again. I'm so sorry, sweetheart. I thought you'd be safe here."

"No, no. It's not that." She pulled back to look at him, not caring that her cheeks were wet. "I was scared that he'd kill me and I'd never get chance to tell you how I feel. Which is daft since we only just... you know. And with this whole 'humans can't know about us or they die' thing you have going." Once the words started, she couldn't stop them. They spilled out of her like water from a broken bucket.

He reached up, putting a finger over her lips to shut her up. His expression was wary as he watched her. "How do you feel, Kacie?"

This was it, crunch time. Taking a deep breath, she looked him in the eye.

"I love you."

There, it was out in the open. She tensed, waiting for him to say something. Perhaps she'd gotten it all wrong? Perhaps he was just looking for a fling before moving on? He was some kind of bear royalty, wasn't he? Perhaps they didn't like bear kings marrying plain old humans...

"Thank fuck," he breathed, dropping his head back and closing his eyes as a look of sheer relief crossed his face. When he looked back at her, his eyes blazed with emotion. "I'll never let anyone hurt you. Ever. I promise."

"What about this rule about I have to marry a bear?" She lifted her chin to look him in the eye. "You going to find me a furry groom as well?"

The tiniest smile lifted the corner of his lips and his voice was rough when he replied. "Yeah. Me."

"Dean Sterling. Was that a proposal?"

Her fingers ghosted over his shoulders. His bare shoulders. Her little start and aborted look downward before she forced herself to keep looking at him made him grin broadly.

"Well, I am on my knees. Which I believe is fairly traditional for a proposal."

"Yes," she hissed. "But you're not supposed to be *naked*!"

He shrugged and pulled her closer until they were pressed together chest to thigh. "So, how about it, Kacie? You're my fated mate, my one and only... I love you, have for years. Will you make me the happiest bear alive and be my wife?"

There was only one answer she could possibly give.

"Oh hell yes!"

"I HAD no idea this was even up here. It's so cute!"

Dean smiled as Kacie went into raptures over the little cabin. High up in forest-covered hills above the town, it was well off the beaten track and isolated. Perfect for a newly mated couple. Correction, he added mentally as he leaned a hip against the counter, watching his little human fated explore... it was perfect for a couple *about* to be mated. Tonight. If he could last that long.

He stayed where he was, arms folded over his chest, just watching for a moment. He still couldn't believe she was here. He'd known for years she was his fated mate, but she was human... and a mating between a Prime and a human? Elitist pricks like Anderson would have kittens. With a mental growl at himself, he put the thought from his mind. He'd let worrying about what other people thought keep him from the love of his life for too long. That was all over.

Sunlight streamed through the windows, catching her in its rays as she flitted around, straightening cushions and touching the small ornaments on the mantelpiece. The photos of him as a child seemed to fascinate her. This had been his family's cabin since he'd been a kid, so there were a lot of them around. He'd never bothered to clear them out when his parents had passed. It hadn't seemed right.

"You were handsome, even back then."

Her soft comment made him smile. "Yeah? I'm surprised you remember."

She put the picture down and turned. The look in her eyes, sultry and dark, made him suck a hard breath in, and that wasn't the only thing that was hard. His cock leapt to attention, ready for action in a heartbeat.

"Well, you know… a gal has to watch her guy."

He'd been going to wait until tonight, really he had. He'd promised himself that he'd do this right. A candlelit meal, rose petals on the bed—he'd even bought the damn rose petals, they were in his truck —but the instant she looked at him like that, all bets were off.

"You weren't the only one watching," he whispered, leaning down to feather his lips over hers. She murmured, a soft sound of pleasure, and moved into his embrace. Wrapping his arms around her, he used his hand at the back of her neck to tilt her lips up to the perfect angle for his kiss.

Keeping it light was out of the question. As soon as her lips parted beneath his, all the years of control, of staying away from her broke, and he surged forward, sliding his tongue deep to taste her.

A low growl rumbled in his chest as he walked her backward toward the single bedroom. She went easily, her trust humbling, but it was her kiss that almost brought him to his knees. Hot, open-mouthed and passionate, she held nothing back. Her small hands tugged at his shirt, pulling it up with impatience.

"I think we've waited long enough then, don't you?" She broke away with a pant, watching as he peeled the shirt off over his head to drop it unheeded on the floor. Lifting her hand, she beckoned him as she backed up with a sexy look on her face. His growl slipped free this time and he stalked her, need and desire surging through his body. The world reduced down to just the cabin and the two of them. Down to the next step he took, with all the speed his werebear physiology was capable of, and swept her back up into his arms. She squealed in delight and clung to his shoulders as he carried her through the door, kicking it shut behind them.

"You're mine, Kacie, you always have been. You just didn't know it," he rumbled softly. "And tonight I'm going to prove it to you."

OH HELL YES. Finally.

Kacie melted at the look in Dean's eyes as he set her down carefully by the side of the bed. The clear hazel was muddied with need, longing and a deep, dark heat that made her shiver. He didn't speak. Didn't need to. The tension that rose between them said all that needed to be said. She lifted on her tiptoes to kiss him, reveling in the differences in their sizes. He'd always been well-built, his body the subject of much subtle, and some not too subtle, ogling from the women in the town. But now she got to feel those muscles up close and personal. Got to run her hands over his broad chest, exploring the solid width of his shoulders before running her hands lower across a stomach with abs as hard as cobblestones.

He groaned and grabbed her hand, shoving it down against the hard erection pressing against his jeans at the same time his mouth crashed down over hers. She moaned, the sound lost into his mouth. A thrill shot through her as she traced his length and girth. He was huge. Way bigger than she expected. A thrill of nervousness raced through her, tempered with sheer desire. She couldn't wait to feel him filling her.

He broke from her lips to trail a hot line of kisses along her jaw and up her neck, hands pulling her shirt from her jeans. She wriggled to help him. Within seconds, the shirt was gone. A sigh escaped her as his hands, large and warm, stroked across her bare skin and then slid upward to cup her breasts. Lazy heat rolled through her body as she arched her back, offering more of herself to him.

"So soft and delicate." His voice was hoarse and full of need as he nuzzled behind her ear. "Beautiful."

Her knees weakened as need shot through her, arrowing down to her core. His touch affected her like no man's had before. She was no innocent, had

had boyfriends before, but it had always felt like something was missing. Now she knew what. They hadn't been Dean. It was like her body had been made for him and reacted only to his touch.

Her hands shook as she found his belt buckle, trying to undo it to get his pants off. She wanted them naked and on the bed, preferably yesterday. A growl slipped from her lips as she couldn't get the leather to work loose.

"Help. I want you naked," she whispered, dropping a kiss on his bare shoulder. Then, driven by instincts she didn't understand, she nipped him lightly.

Nothing could have prepared her for the response she got. A deep snarl rolled up from the center of his chest and the next moment she found herself flat on her back on the bed with Dean braced over her.

"How about I get you naked first...and then I'm going to make you scream my name."

Oh god.

Unable to answer with more than a nod, she gasped as he pulled at her jeans. He didn't undo them, instead, the sound of tearing fabric filled the air and suddenly the denim, and her panties, slid down her legs. Heat hit her cheeks but she ignored it, twisting her arms behind her back to unclip her bra. Sliding it free, she dropped it over the side of the bed and lay back.

Warily, she watched his face as his gaze swept up from her bare feet all the way up. Would he like what he saw? She'd seen his girlfriends over the years… all from out of town; blonde and leggy. Everything she wasn't. The impulse to move, to cover herself with her hands, almost won out. But as soon as she started to move, he was there.

"No." His voice was hard as he grabbed her wrists and held her arms out to the side. "Never hide yourself from me. You're beautiful…and all mine."

"Ohhh… *god, yes…*" she managed as he slid down her body, using a hard knee to part her thighs before he slid between them. His hot breath on her inner thigh made her jump before he parted her gently with his thumbs. Her body tensed, anticipation almost killing her, and then he swept his tongue over her and her hips jerked off the bed. Liquid heat escaped her, bringing another flush to her cheeks at how easily her needy body responded to him. Would he think she was easy?

But he growled in approval, hands hard on her hips as he feasted with abandon. Whimpers filled the air and she writhed as he nibbled and licked at her clit. He moved down to tease the entrance to her body with his clever tongue, circling it before he thrust inside and she lost her voice. He alternated fucking her with hot, fast stabs of his tongue and torturing her clit with hard licks and nibbles until she thought she'd go out of her mind.

Tension built up in her core, so tight she wasn't sure she could take anymore, that she would shatter apart any second, but she didn't. He played her body, teased her reactions and filled her senses while holding her right on the edge of pleasure. But it wasn't enough. Would never be enough. She needed him over her, within her, covering her even as he filled her over and over again.

"Please... Dean..." she begged, reaching for him. She was done with his teasing. "I need you. Just you. Please."

He left off his sensual torture, the sound of tearing denim loud in the room as he got rid of his jeans. Then he was back, leaving a trail of kisses as he crawled up her body. Each one made her shudder, her body no longer her own. Passing her breasts, he licked over her nipples with lazy swipes of his tongue and then braced himself over her to claim her lips in a carnal, open-mouth kiss.

She moaned, clinging to him. He was huge,

bigger and harder than she was, heavily muscled. She'd never thought of herself as a typical woman, so the primal instincts that thrilled at his dominant manner took her by surprise, but she liked it. Liked the way he held her—protective and possessive. Like she was the most delicate thing in the world, to be protected and... all his.

He moved without warning, holding her close to turn them over so that she sat in his lap. His face was tight as he looked up at her. "Easier this way. You have more control."

She easily read his worries. "Shhh, I'm a big girl. You won't hurt me. I promise."

He didn't move, still watching her.

She frowned, wariness creeping into her. "What is it? What's wrong?"

"Bears..." he seemed to struggle with the words. "When bears mate, there's... it's different from human marriage, love. There are no words. Instead..." He sighed. "I'm sorry, Kacie, but I have to bite you."

Her eyebrows shot up. "Bite? Not as in love nips, I take it?"

He shook his head, worry in his eyes. "Bite, bite. I have to leave a mark on your shoulder. Then everyone knows you're mine for always. No divorce, no nothing."

Her surprise filtered away under an onslaught of warmth. He'd always be hers then. The ultimate commitment.

"Go on then... I know you won't hurt me."

Surprise filled his eyes, his nostrils flaring suddenly. Heat followed and he nodded, decision obviously made.

Reaching between them, he fisted his cock, pumping the rigid length a few times before fitting the broad head against the entrance to her body. He checked her face again before easing her over him. Sinking down, she groaned as his thick intrusion parted her pussy lips... then stopped.

"Oh fuck, you're tight." He groaned, pulling back before pushing upward again. Large hands spread out over her hips. Biting her lip, she tried to relax as he fed his cock into her, seesawing so he slid into her a little more each time. Finally, he was buried in her to the hilt, her pussy throbbing as it stretched tightly around him.

His eyes were dark as he reached up to pull her down for a kiss, his tongue driving as deeply into her as his cock was in her cunt. She whimpered as he stroked her, teasing her and tempting her to join the erotic dance. She did, winding her tongue around his.

Then he started to move. He rocked his hips just a fraction, and sensation exploded within her. He held her close as she rode him, slowly at first but with increasing speed. His hips rocked, each thrust upward stroking nerve endings that sang in pleasure at his touch. She couldn't hold in her gasps, her hands spread out over his strong arms as he impaled her on his thick cock again and again. Giving up all pretense of control, she let him lead the way, using his strength to control their motion and bring them both pleasure.

Time had no meaning as they moved together, her hair a dark cloud around them as she leaned down to claim his mouth again. He kissed like he fucked—hard and demanding but with an edge of sweetness she knew she'd never get enough of. The tension and need in her body escalated, her movements becoming jerky as she reached the edge.

"Dean," she whispered, breaking away to whisper against his lips. "I love you."

"I love you too, sweetheart," he rumbled again, a bear sound of pure pleasure as he kissed along her jaw feverishly and then along her shoulder. "Now come for me."

His hold tightened as he thrust up again, rolling his hips to grind his pelvis against hers. The movement trapped her clit between them, and she moaned in pleasure. At the same time, he bit her, sinking sharp teeth deep into the fleshy part of her shoulder and claiming her with his body and his soul.

Ecstasy exploded through her as her climax hit hard and fast. He growled as her pussy gripped his cock, milking him in her pleasure, and he sped up. Holding her still, he took her with a power and precision that fed the release that rolled through her. Hard thrusts claimed her, body and soul.

Then his rhythm broke down, and his thrusts became uncoordinated. Breaking from her shoulder, he slammed into her a last time, throwing back his head and roaring his release as his cock pumped his seed deep within her. She felt every pulse and jerk, murmuring in pleasure as she wrapped herself around him.

They stayed that way for long minutes, their bodies coming down from the high. His big hands stroked idly over her back until, finally, he lifted his head to look at her. Love filled her at the look on his face—totally contented and at peace. Leaning forward, she placed a gentle kiss on his lips. He was hers, and she was his. After years being apart, they'd finally found one another.

But that didn't mean she was finished yet. A twinkle in her eye, she sat back, rocking her hips so that his still hard cock slid within her tightness.

"Now, I believe someone promised to…" she paused to grin, "Bear up and show me some stamina…"

YOU MIGHT ALSO LIKE...

WANT MORE BEARS FROM BEAUTY?

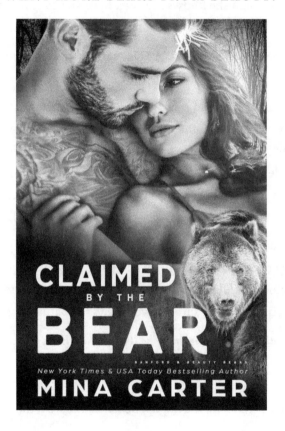

Tall, dark and handsome, she's watched him from afar for years...

Back in the small town of Beauty after a broken engagement, Kaitlyn Turner has two things on her mind: regaining her independence and having a good night out with her bestie. Only somehow, their celebrations include hitting up the local tattoo parlour. The Tattoo parlour run by Creed, her late brothers best friend. Hot as Hades, he's the one man she knows she can't have, but the one she'd kill to have look at her as more than a kid sister.

Petite, curvy, beautiful...and human. She's everything he wants, and everything he can't have.

Werebear Creed is a loner in the Beauty pack. Tall, powerfully built, and mean as hell, he holds rank as an enforcer despite the fact his bear prefers to stay well hidden. No matter, he can enforce pack rules in human form... even against fully shifted bears. They might call him a half-skin but no one wants to piss him off. Ever.

He doesn't care what they think. Until Kaitlyn Turner walks back into town. He's wanted her for years, but she's human and he's a bear. No can do. But then an attack brings her over into his world and the path is clear.

She's always been his...now he'll claim her. Even if he has to fight the whole pack to do so...

minacarter.com/index.php/book/claimed-by-the-bear

ABOUT THE AUTHOR

Mina Carter is a *New York Times & USA Today* bestselling author of romance in many genres. She lives in the UK with her husband, daughter and a bossy cat.

Connect with Mina online at:
minacarter.com

WANT THE LATEST NEWS AND CONTESTS?

SIGN UP TO MINA'S NEWSLETTER!

facebook.com/minacarterauthor

twitter.com/minacarter

instagram.com/minacarter77

bookbub.com/profile/mina-carter

CPSIA information can be obtained
at www.ICGtesting.com
Printed in the USA
BVHW071402051119
562962BV00007B/22/P